"The worst thing is," Emma said,

"is that even though I believe him when he says he didn't do it, there's one small part of me that wonders if he was involved somehow." Emma looked down at her white-knuckled hands and tried to relax. "I hate myself for thinking that!"

Darcy spoke up for the first time. "Emma, you don't have anything to worry about. The only thing Kurt's stolen is your heart."

"How can you be so sure?" Sam challenged her. "Emma says his fingerprints were on everything."

"I just know," Darcy said matter-of-factly.

"What are you, psychic?" Sam asked.

"Not exactly," Darcy answered . . .

The SUNSET ISLAND series
by Cherie Bennett

Sunset Scandal

CHERIE BENNETT

SPLASH™

A BERKLEY / SPLASH BOOK

For Jeff, upon whom I base all the coolest of male characters

ONE

"Whew, I'm beat," Emma Cresswell announced, throwing herself down on her bed.

"Me, too," agreed Carrie Alden, plopping into the chair near Emma's dresser.

"These hands were not meant for manual labor," Samantha Bridges groaned from her spot on the carpet. "Even my blisters have blisters."

The three best friends had just returned from a full day of helping to clean up the damage resulting from Hurricane Julius, which had hit Sunset Island a few days earlier.

"I need a long, hot shower." Emma sighed. "If only I had the energy to stand up and get these muddy clothes off!"

"I'll second that," Carrie agreed.

1

"Hey, we need a serious attitude adjustment here," Sam objected. "Remember, we have a party to go to tonight."

"Party?" Carrie groaned. "I just want to crawl into bed."

"I bet Billy would like that idea," Sam said with a wink, referring to Billy Sampson, Carrie's boyfriend, "but maybe you and he should dance a few numbers first."

"I love dancing with Kurt," Emma murmured dreamily. "Actually, I love *everything* with Kurt," she added, smiling up at the ceiling.

Emma had fallen in love with Kurt Ackerman the summer before, her first summer as an au pair on Sunset Island. Emma had met Kurt at the Sunset Country Club, where she'd taken Katie Hewitt, the little girl in her charge, for her swimming lessons. Kurt was working his way through college as a swimming instructor there. After a turbulent romance—they'd even broken up at the end of the summer—Emma and Kurt were back together again. And nothing could have made Emma happier. Correction: the one thing that would make her happier would be if Kurt could stop minding that she had been born rich, while he had to work for every penny he had. If that happened, things would be totally perfect.

"Yeah, yeah, love is grand and all that," Sam said breezily, picking herself up from the carpet. "I'd better get back to the Jacobses' and get cleaned up for the Flirts' party."

Flirting with Danger—or the Flirts, as the band was commonly called—was a very hot rock band that was rapidly gaining a national following. They were giving a party that night at the Play Café, the local club where everyone hung out. They were calling it a post-hurricane blowout, and had told everyone to come in their wildest hurricane outfits.

"What are you going to wear?" Emma asked, sitting up.

Sam shrugged and headed for the door. "Something scandalous."

"Oh, hey, you have to see this," Emma said, jumping off the bed. She opened her closet and sorted through the dozens of hangers. "My father's fiancée sent me an

3

outfit. It's . . . indescribable. Wait until you see it."

"It was nice of her to send you something, though," Carrie said, resting her chin on her hands. Both she and Sam knew Emma couldn't stand Valerie, her stepmother-to-be, and thought she dressed like an over-aged, bleached-blond Minnie Mouse.

"You may change your mind when you see it," Emma said, laughing. "Ah, here it is!" She pulled the hanger from the closet and held up the outfit for inspection.

Sam and Carrie were speechless. Emma was holding a short yellow polyester sun-dress with pink bows marching over it in every direction. The neckline, sleeves, and hem were festooned with rows of pink lace ruffles.

"She isn't serious," Carrie said. "Is she?"

"Wait, wait, it gets even better!" Emma cried. She lifted up the skirt to reveal a matching pair of ruffled and bow-covered short shorts.

"That's the funniest thing I've ever seen!" Sam hooted.

"Oh, you should definitely wear it," Carrie added. "It's so . . . so you!"

Emma laughed. What it definitely was *not*

was her, and her friends knew that only too well. Understated, elegant clothes suited Emma's perfect blond bob, classic features, and graceful, slender figure better. And fortunately for her, she had the bucks to dress exactly as she wanted.

"You know," Sam said, eyeing the outfit critically, "if you took the ruffles off the shorts and wore them with, oh, say, a pink bra top and cowboy boots, it would be hot."

Emma smiled. "Sam, you're talking about something *you* would wear, not something *I* would wear."

"Was I?" Sam asked innocently.

"Take it," Emma said, thrusting the hanger at Sam.

"You amaze me," Carrie told Sam. "You can come up with the wildest combinations of clothes, and they always work."

"It's a gift," Sam agreed, taking the hanger from Emma. "I'll wear this to the party tonight, in honor of Valerie!" Sam waved and bounded down the stairs.

"Can you imagine if I dressed like that?" Carrie asked Emma. "I'd look like a refugee from the circus." She stood up and stretched, then reached down and touched her toes. "God, I really *am* sore."

"It was those last few hours picking up the debris from the shoreline that probably did it," Emma said sympathetically. "You were really working hard."

"So were you. So was everyone," Carrie said. She walked over to the bed and plopped down. "It was really terrible by the shacks, wasn't it?" she said quietly.

"It was," Emma agreed. She stared thoughtfully at her friend. Not long before the hurricane, Carrie had been offered an opportunity to have some of her photographs published in a book about Sunset Island. Kurt, who had been raised on the island, had taken Carrie on a tour of some of the less well known sites so she could photograph them. One of the places he'd taken her was the poorest neighborhood on the island. It was no more than some shacks and hovels right near a fetid swamp. Carrie had been shocked to find out that such conditions existed on Sunset Island, where many rich, famous people had summer homes. The publisher had refused to include those photos in the book, and Carrie had bowed out of the project.

Emma had been truly touched by Carrie's decision. And like Carrie, now that she knew what things were really like, she felt compelled to try to do something about it.

"Those people from COPE are amazing, aren't they?" Emma mused.

Carrie nodded. "They worked so hard, and they were so kind to those little kids whose families lost their homes." Kurt had introduced Carrie to some of the people from COPE—or Citizens of Positive Ethics. It was their organization that was working diligently to help the poor people on the island.

"I'm going to join, I think," Emma said quietly. It would be a big step for her. Not a joiner by nature, she would have found it easier just to write a big, fat check and let other people do the dirty work. But that, she had decided, would be too easy. Besides, if she was completely honest with herself, the fact that Kurt was so involved with them was a factor as well. She knew Kurt would approve of her decision and would admire her for it.

"Me, too," Carrie agreed. "There's a meeting tomorrow night, you know," she added.

Emma nodded. She knew Kurt would be there. "Let's go," she said firmly, then added, "What about Sam? Do you think she'll want to come, too?"

"Tough to say." Carrie shrugged. "I mean, she's got a heart as big as the world, but then she can be really . . . I don't know . . . pragmatic sometimes, you know?"

Emma nodded again thoughtfully. Sam had been all for Carrie having her photographs in the Sunset Island book, even if the publisher did want to edit out all the pictures that showed the not-so-pretty side of the island. According to Sam, Emma knew, as long as you didn't have to do anything really illegal or immoral, you should "go for the gusto."

"I'll ask Sam tonight if she wants to join us," Emma decided.

"Good," Carrie approved, brushing her long brown hair out of her eyes. She got up, picked up her purse, and slung it over her shoulder. "I'm heading for the world's longest, steamiest shower. See you tonight!"

After Carrie left, Emma got into the

shower herself. As she shampooed her hair she thought again how terrific everything was with Kurt. And how terrible she had felt when they'd broken up. *I'll never let anything come between us again*, she vowed to herself as she rinsed her hair.

Not that it was any fault of hers that they had broken up in the first place. Oh, it had been her decision all right, but not only had Kurt gone out with her archenemy, Diana De Witt, he had actually *slept* with her. Just remembering how betrayed she had felt was like sticking a knife into her heart all over again. *She* hadn't even slept with Kurt yet, because she wanted to make sure that the time was absolutely right.

Actually, I'm still not sure, Emma thought with a small smile. She turned the hot water on even hotter and let it pound against her face. Once they'd gotten back together, she had decided that "go slow" would be her motto. Still, maybe the infamous right time was coming soon. . . .

"Wow, Emma, you look pretty!" five-year-old Katie told Emma when she came downstairs dressed for the party.

"Thanks," Emma said, kneeling down to hug the little girl.

"Katie's right, per usual," Jane Hewitt said, walking into the hall. Jane and Jeff Hewitt were Emma's employers for the second summer in a row. Both lawyers in their mid-thirties, they had a great relationship and three super kids. Twelve-year-old Ethan, who had had a crush on Emma the summer before, was the oldest. Then there was freckle-faced Wills, a seven-year-old ball of energy, and five-year-old Katie, who was as smart as she was darling. Emma had come to love the entire family, and they seemed to feel the same way about her.

Jeff Hewitt came up behind his wife and put his arms around her. "Remember, Jane, when you said that miniskirts would never come back into style because women would never put up with how impractical they were?" he asked in a teasing voice.

Jane rolled her eyes. "So I'm no predictor of fashion," she said. "I gave away all my miniskirts shortly after the sixties ended."

"And now you have to go out and buy more that look exactly like the ones you gave to Goodwill!" Jeff exclaimed.

"Fortunately I'm better at law than I am at guessing fashion trends," Jane said ruefully.

"Don't tell anyone, Em," Jeff said conspiratorially, "but Jane wore hers a lot shorter at your age than you do!"

Jane laughed. "You're much saner than I was, Emma—thank God!"

Emma smiled warmly at them. They were really so terrific.

"You're still pretty wild, in your own lawyerlike way," Jeff said, kissing his wife's cheek.

"Kisses for me, too, Daddy!" Katie said, running up to hug her father's knees. He hoisted her quickly and covered her cheek with loud kisses. Jane kissed the little girl from the other side.

Suddenly Emma felt her throat close up. Jane and Jeff loved each other and their kids so much. Emma had lived with them long enough to know that their closeness was no artifice put on for public consumption.

That was what Emma had thought it had to be, at first. After all, coming from her unhappy home, how was she to know there really were genuinely loving families around? Her parents had been in the middle of an ugly divorce for an eternity, and both were engaged to people closer to Emma's age than to their own. Even before the breakup, they'd never shown any real affection to each other. *Nor to me*, Emma added to herself bitterly. They had showered her with money instead.

Okay, enough of this melodrama, she told herself. *You're on your way to a party with the cutest, greatest guy in the world, so snap out of it!*

Emma drove Jane's car to the other side of the island, where Kurt lived with his father and his two younger sisters. He had had his own apartment for a brief period, but had opted to move back home to save money. Emma had never met Kurt's family but knew that his mother had died of cancer when Kurt was in high school.

Emma pulled into the narrow driveway and eyed the small frame house. Her gaze fell on the other houses lining the narrow lane, where fishermen's families lived their lives. This was a world where buying a new dress or a pair of shoes had to be planned and budgeted for. This was a world where a vacation meant a stroll on the beach and where a car was kept until it just wouldn't run anymore. To Emma, this was a foreign country.

"You are one gorgeous sight," Kurt said with a big grin when Emma knocked on the front screen door.

"I must have washed a bucketful of mud off myself," Emma said, laughing.

Kurt opened the screen door and gave Emma a kiss. "You taste good, too," he added.

"Your chariot awaits," Emma said, sweeping her hand toward the BMW in the driveway. Kurt always picked her up when they went out, but his car had broken down and was in the shop.

"Much fancier than my chariot," Kurt noted. "Bye, Dad, I'm going!" he called into the recesses of the house.

A weathered older man appeared from around a corner, wiping his hands on a dishtowel.

Why, he looks just like Kurt! Emma thought. *But older and tired. No*, she corrected herself as he walked toward her, *he looks like an old, tired, suspicious Kurt*.

"Dad, this is my girlfriend, Emma Cresswell," Kurt said, introducing her. "Emma, this is my dad."

"It's a pleasure to meet you," Emma said in her cultured voice. She winced inwardly. Even to her own ears, she sounded like she'd just stepped out of an elite finishing school.

"Hmph," Mr. Ackerman said, eyeing Emma.

For once, poised Emma didn't have a clue as to what to say. *"You have a nice house"?* But that was ridiculous—the house was a tiny frame bungalow that looked like all the others on the street. *"You raised a great son"? "Sorry your wife died"? "Your son is a terrific kisser"?*

"Well, we have to go," Kurt said, saving the moment.

"I . . . I'm glad we finally met," Emma managed. She looked at Kurt. "Your son means a lot to me," she added.

"He means a lot to me, too," Mr. Ackerman said levelly, then he nodded and headed back to the kitchen.

"Did I say something wrong?" Emma asked Kurt when they got into the car. "He hates me!"

"He doesn't hate you," Kurt explained. "He's just . . . I guess you could say he's protective of me."

Emma backed the car out of the driveway. "Well, then, he should be happy that you're happy, shouldn't he?"

"He just needs time to get to know you," Kurt said soothingly, "and when he does, he'll see why I'm so crazy about you."

Emma gave Kurt an arch look. "Is that so?"

"That's so," he affirmed. He put his arm under her hair and stroked the back of her neck.

"Mmm, that feels great," Emma sighed. She stopped for a red light and looked over at him. "Carrie and I had a talk today after we left you," she told him. "We're both planning to join COPE tomorrow."

Kurt's face lit up with admiration. "Really? That's great!"

Emma smiled back at Kurt as the light turned green. She loved him so much. He was such a good person—a really moral guy who cared about people. *He's also incredibly hot-looking*, she added to herself with a secret smile.

"I'm really proud of you, Emma," Kurt said. "I mean, someone like you, you could just write a check and not get involved in the dirty work."

"I want to do more than that," Emma said seriously. She wasn't about to tell him that she had certainly considered doing exactly that—just writing a check. She hoped she was joining because it meant something to her, and not just to see that look of pride on Kurt's face.

TWO

"This place is packed!" Emma said to Kurt as they squeezed through the crowded doorway of the Play Café.

"And how!" Kurt said, smiling back. "Looks like most everyone survived the storm. Including a few people who should have been swept out to sea."

Kurt pointed to a broad, leather-jacketed back just inside the front door. It was Butchie, one of the guys Kurt had gone to high school with—an all-around nasty dude. The previous summer, Butchie had passed the time intimidating people at the pool table—until he had been out-hustled unexpectedly by Carrie, who had decided to teach Butchie a lesson and had surprised them all with her skill.

"Forget Butchie," Emma said lightly. "Look! There's Sam and Carrie." She motioned to a table under one of the Play Café's rock-video monitors.

It took Emma and Kurt some time, though, to work their way through the crush of bodies toward their friends. It seemed that half the island had turned out for the party, and apparently they all had stories to tell about Hurricane Julius, because everyone was jabbering away at a million miles an hour.

The deejay, meanwhile, was spinning an assortment of classic rock tunes that all seemed to have a storm theme. Emma picked out an Allman Brothers version of "Stormy Monday," the Doors' "Riders on the Storm," and Bob Dylan's "Idiot Wind." A bunch of people were already boogieing away on the café's tiny dance floor.

Kurt took Emma's hand and gave it a squeeze. Emma squeezed back. *What a scene!* she thought.

Finally they made it over to Carrie and Sam's table. In keeping with the theme of the party, Carrie was wearing a cute short yellow rain slicker imprinted with tiny blue umbrellas, and a pair of black capri tights. Sam had on the short shorts that Valerie had given to Emma and the pink bra top she had described. And pinned to the bra top—in honor of their nickname for Emma's father's young fiancée—was a Minnie Mouse pin.

Emma cracked up when she saw Sam's outfit. "Sam Bridges, you are a total original," she said. "You look great, too, Carrie. I didn't know you owned that slicker."

Carrie looked sheepish. "My mother stuck it in the bottom of my suitcase before I left. She'd heard it rains a lot in Maine. She should have been here a few days ago!"

Sam reached for the tall glass of ginger ale that was on the table in front of her. "Don't look now, *compadres*," she said, "but my sensors are detecting the approach of radioactive alien life forms."

Emma looked in the direction Sam was nodding. Approaching the table were none other than Lorell Courtland and Diana De Witt.

Ever since Emma, Carrie, and Sam had arrived on Sunset Island, they'd had trouble with Lorell and Diana. Emma had attended boarding school with Diana in Switzerland, and the two girls had held each other in contempt for years. It wasn't any better on the island. They'd met Lorell at the international au pair convention in New York the previous year, where Lorell had shown herself to be a pampered and supercilious social climber.

As luck would have it, Lorell and Diana were old friends. Both were also gorgeous. Diana had curly chestnut hair, blue eyes, and a perfect figure, while Lorell was slender with aquiline features and glossy dark hair cut in a crisp bob.

Oh, great, Emma thought as she watched Lorell and Diana approach them. *Just what the doctor ordered to screw up a great night.* A vision of Kurt and Diana locked in a passionate embrace flashed before her eyes. *That's what they must have looked like when they were together,* she thought miserably remembering their brief fling the previous summer. *Stop that!* Emma commanded herself. But the image lingered even though she tried to will it away.

"Well, well," Lorell drawled, her Georgia accent even thicker than normal, "if it isn't the guilty-conscience brigade! You know the whole island's talking about how you do-good creatures got your hands all dirty tryin'—and failin'—to save those rundown hovels."

"So much work for nothing!" Diana cooed with false compassion. She eyed Kurt meaningfully. "But Kurt, it seems to have made your body even leaner and more muscled than I remember! Of course," she added insinuatingly, "it *is* difficult to tell with all your clothes on."

Kurt took Emma's hand protectively, and Emma felt fire start to shoot from her eyes.

"Well, Diana," Sam said cheerfully, jumping to her friend's defense, "from what I hear, you've seen just about the entire male population of the state of Maine without clothes on. It must get hard to differentiate after a while."

Diana looked at Sam archly. "Oh no, I only bother with the really interesting ones," Diana said coolly, "such as a certain bass player from Flirting with Danger."

Diana could only be referring to Presley Travis, Sam's partner in flirtation and sometime boyfriend. "Listen, you dirtbag—" Sam began hotly.

"Ta-ta, kiddies!" Lorell trilled, leading Diana away.

"What a bitch," Kurt moaned in disbelief, burying his head in his hands.

"Oh no you don't," Emma said, tugging gently on Kurt's hair. "I want everyone to see that you're here with me."

"Hey, look what just blew in the door!" Sam said, pointing through the crowd. "It's Trent!"

Sam was referring to Trent Hayden-Bishop III, Emma's socially correct "boyfriend" with whom she had attended society parties when she was growing up. Emma had never really thought of him as more than a friend, though Trent had professed to be devastated when she told him that. Trent and Sam had gone out a couple of times the previous summer, though Sam, too, didn't find him all that hot. Rich, but not hot.

"Who's that with him?" Carrie asked, craning her neck for a better look.

"It's Daphne Whittinger!" Emma said with surprise. "At least I think it's Daphne. She looks great!"

"Trent and Daphne a couple?" Sam said. "Unbelievable!"

"They're coming right this way," Emma sighed. *Just what I need*, she thought. *The anorexic, diet pilled-out girl who tried to slash me last summer and the old boyfriend whom I never loved.*

Emma knew that Daphne had gone into treatment, and had even seen her briefly when Daphne had apologized to her at their spring break party on the island. As Daphne and Trent came closer Emma had to admit that Daphne looked much healthier.

"Trent! Daphne! Will wonders never cease!" Sam said, laughing. "Did you two get hooked up on *Love Connection?*"

"Hi, all," Trent said in his breezy, upper-crust Boston accent. "Hi, Emma," he added.

Trent looks just the same, Emma thought, looking at his slender five-foot-ten frame and his blandly handsome face topped by brown hair cut short in the back, long in the front. It was the standard rich-boy, preppy hair cut, and Trent wore the standard rich-boy, preppy clothes. But then, that was Trent. As far as Emma could see, he didn't have an original bone in his body.

But Daphne—could it be true? Emma thought. *She's definitely put on some weight. She actually looks almost normal. Her clothes don't just hang on her body anymore.*

Daphne smiled and took Trent's hand. "Trent and I are both in recovery," she said to all of them. "We met again at a twelve-step group."

The girls and Kurt looked at one another in wonder. Could Daphne actually be telling the truth?

"Yeah," Trent added. "It's true. I decided that I had to get my drinking under control or else I would ruin my life." He looked over at Daphne. "And Daphne decided that she had to get her anorexia under control. We met at a clinic that helps people with a lot of different problems. Now we go to twelve-step meetings together."

Daphne smiled again. "It's wonderful to have my life together again. I was a jerk last summer. I was worse than a jerk. But I have a new life now. Will you forgive me?" She looked directly at Emma.

Emma noticed that Daphne's smile never left her face. *What can I say?* Emma thought. *I don't exactly trust her, but I don't*

24

want to be a bitch, either. And what's with that smile?

"Of course, Daphne," Emma replied graciously. "I'm glad you're feeling better about yourself. You too, Trent."

"Great!" Daphne said, still smiling. "I hope we all get to be true friends. Let's go dance, Trent. I think the Flirts are ready to start playing."

The girls and Kurt watched them leave. "Wow," Carrie said. "That's the last thing I expected to see tonight."

Kurt spoke up. "I think it's great," he said. "Don't forget how messed-up she was last summer."

"How could I?" Emma asked. Daphne had been so zoned up on diet pills that she'd thought Emma was out to get her, and had attacked her with a shard of broken glass. It had been a total nightmare.

"I didn't even know Trent had a drinking problem," Carrie said.

"Neither did I," Emma admitted. "I mean, I knew he drank a lot, but so do a lot of people. That doesn't make them alcoholics."

"Sometimes the person doing the drinking

is the last one to know," Sam said meaning-fully.

Emma got the message. When the prob-lems with her parents had gotten worse, she'd starting drinking wine. It had seemed like nothing at first, just a way to relax. But she knew now she'd been very close to being out of control. Luckily, with the help of her friends, she had stopped.

"I'm going to get some more popcorn," Kurt said, giving Emma a kiss. "I'll be right back."

After he was out of hearing range, Carrie and Sam started in on Emma about him. Sam chanted in a singsong voice, "First comes love, then comes marriage, then comes—"

"He's crazy about you, you know," Carrie chimed in. "Did you see how embarrassed he was when Diana stopped by?"

Emma smiled dreamily. "I think he's the greatest. And what he did for those poor people during the hurricane—I'll remember it for the rest of my life."

"Which reminds me," Carrie said to Emma, "we were going to tell Sam about that COPE meeting tomorrow night, right?"

"Right," Emma said, turning to Sam.

"There's a hurricane recovery meeting. Carrie and I are going, and we need all the help we can get. There's a lot of work to do."

Sam laughed. "I surrender! I'll come with you. How can I resist? I mean, what if Diana and Lorell decide to show up? You'd need someone to protect you."

"Now why is it I don't think those two charmers will show up at a COPE meeting?" Carrie asked, raising her eyebrows.

"Because you have a brain," Sam explained.

Emma and Carrie grinned at each other. *Samantha Bridges at a COPE meeting tomorrow night—it must be a full moon,* Emma thought.

"Okay, okay, enough politics," Sam said. "Let's go break a few hearts." And she led her friends out to the dance floor.

The next morning, Emma was straightening the Hewitts' kitchen after breakfast when Katie's voice called from the front hall.

"Emma!" Katie sang out. "Mail's here!"

Emma turned the sink tap off and went into the hall to gather the mail. She flipped through it disinterestedly. Mostly bills for the Hewitts and junk mail. Then she stopped and stared at one envelope addressed to her in elegant calligraphy. *No return address. An invitation,* she thought. *But from whom?*

Emma tore open the envelope and scanned the invitation. *I can't believe it,* she thought. *It's an invitation to my mother and Austin Payne's engagement party. And the party's going to be right here on the island, at the Sunset Country Club. On Tuesday! Why, that's less than a week from now!*

Emma simply could not abide her mother's fiancé. Austin Payne was only twenty-five years old. An artist of some renown, he was only after her mother's fortune—Emma was certain of that. She knew Austin fooled around behind her mother's back. She considered him a total snake.

Emma strode right to the telephone and dialed her mother in Boston.

She was surprised when her mother, rather than one of the staff, answered. "Kat Cresswell speaking," came a frosty voice.

"Mother," Emma said, playing with a pen, "it's Emma. I just received the invitation to your engagement party."

"Emma! My secretary sent that invitation to you weeks ago!" Kat exclaimed. "You really should have responded sooner."

"She didn't send it weeks ago," Emma said evenly. "I'm telling you, it just arrived." She looked at the envelope. "It's postmarked the day before yesterday, Mother," she added pointedly.

After a moment of silence, Kat spoke up. "Well, the post office must have made some kind of error."

"Mother," Emma said, "didn't it seem odd to you that I hadn't called you about this?"

"Why, Emma," Kat continued in her animated voice, "I tried to phone you. But there was that silly storm, and then your employers don't have an answering machine."

She's lying to me, Emma thought bitterly. *She never called. In fact, she simply forgot to send me the invitation.* Marshaling all her composure, she said, "I'm not sure I believe you."

"Emma!" her mother exclaimed, a hurt tone in her voice. "Of course I tried."

"Mother, even if you did try, why are you having the party here on Sunset Island?

29

Couldn't you find someplace . . . well, closer to home?" Emma dreaded the idea of her mother's engagement party on what she thought of as *her* island.

"But Emma, Sunset Island is so, well, magical! It will be a magnificent party. Please bring that handsome young man— what's his name?—as your escort. See you at the party!" Kat hung up.

Emma continued to speak into the receiver, though she knew her mother couldn't hear her. "His name is Kurt. And by the way, I loathe the guy you're marrying. Actually, the two of you make me sick."

She had thought that saying it out loud might make her feel better, but somehow it didn't help at all.

That night, at the COPE meeting, Emma met up with Carrie and Sam and told them all about the upcoming engagement party and about the conversation with her mother. She had hoped to tell Kurt about it, too, but he was busy that night driving a taxi—his other part-time job—so he couldn't be at the meeting. Emma was just getting to the part about how her mother had invited her to bring "that handsome young man" whose name she didn't remember when a rap from a gavel silenced the group of approximately sixty people gathered for the meeting.

Jade Meader, the sprightly older woman who was one of the leaders of COPE, rapped the gavel again and called for order.

"Okay, thank you for coming," she said in a strong voice that belied her years. "As you know, we've got a tremendous amount of work to do. For the moment, we're going to put aside our work to stop the developers. Instead, we've got to raise enough money to resettle those poor island residents who lost their homes to the hurricane."

"Good thing their homes weren't worth that much!" Sam quipped in a whisper.

"Shut up!" Emma and Carrie whispered back.

"Now, this is not an easy job," Jade continued. "But we're going to do it—step by step, brick by brick, dollar by dollar!"

"Right on!" someone shouted from the back of the room.

"And we're starting tomorrow," Jade continued in a firm voice. "There's plenty of money on Sunset Island. And we're going to get donations from everyone who lives here. Because we're not going to be afraid to ask." Jade banged the gavel on the lectern for emphasis.

When Jade was done speaking, COPE volunteers went through the crowd, assigning everyone an area for the fundraising drive. Carrie, Emma, and Sam were given official COPE membership cards to show people when asking for contributions, and each got a map of the island with an area circled in red.

"This is where you guys go door-to-door," the volunteer explained to them. "Remember, always be polite, but try to get our message across. And any amount of money is helpful."

"How about we meet at the boardwalk at eight-thirty," Emma told her friends, "and go from there, okay?"

"Eight-thirty? You mean A.M., in the morning, before *noon?*" Sam groaned. "The only thing I want to be doing at that hour is sleeping!"

Emma and Carrie cracked up. "You'll be there, Samantha Bridges or else," Emma warned between giggles.

"Oh yeah? Who's gonna make me?" Sam asked mock-belligerently.

"I am," Emma responded. "I'm picking you up at eight." And she and Carrie started laughing again.

"Don't pick me up," Sam said, "I'm going to jog over. It'll wake me up."

"Are you sure?" Emma began.

"I'm sure, I'm sure!" Sam said.

"Okay, see you tomorrow," Emma said, heading for the Hewitt's car. *Maybe I'll be too busy with COPE work to go to my mother's party*, she thought. But she realized even as she considered this possibility that it was only wishful thinking. She really had to go.

At least I'll be with Kurt, she thought. She closed her eyes and imagined how it felt when he kissed her. A delicious feeling ran through her. Even *thinking* about him made her blood pressure rise!

Hmm, Emma mused as she unlocked the car door, *wouldn't it serve my mother right if I chose the night of her engagement party to lose my virginity?*

That's ridiculous, a second voice in her

head chided. *That's a truly stupid reason to do it.*

"Maybe it is and maybe it isn't," Emma said out loud as she started the car. "Maybe it isn't at all."

THREE

"Hi, hi, hi!" Katie yelled as she ran over to Carrie and Sam, who sat on a bench on the boardwalk the next morning. "I get to help collect money!"

"Good for you," Carrie said, grinning back at the little girl.

"I see you're on duty," Sam said as Emma reached them.

"Jane and Jeff slept in," Emma said, "so I brought Katie along."

"Well, she's so cute, people will probably give you more money," Carrie commented.

Sam raised her sunglasses and eyed Emma's clothes. "What is that, your gracious-lady-collecting-for-charity outfit?"

Emma blushed. Both Carrie and Sam were wearing jeans and T-shirts. She could see now that the off-white linen pants and silk blouse she'd worn were all wrong. The truth of the matter was that her only experience with raising money for charity came from overhearing her mother on the phone soliciting checks from her rich friends for the ballet, or the opera, or something equally tony.

"Hey, it's too early in the morning to rag on Emma," Carrie chided Sam. "Besides," she added to Emma, "you look great."

"I guess I thought I'd look more . . . legit or something if I dressed up," Emma sighed, crowding in on their bench.

Katie cuddled up to Emma. "I think you look like a princess," she said seriously.

Carrie stood up. "We'd better get started. I have to be back in two hours to drive Ian to a dentist appointment. After that I have to drive him back home—he has band practice."

"God, I hope they don't make you stay and listen," Sam said, wincing.

Thirteen-year-old Ian Templeton, one of the two kids Carrie was taking care of, had a band called Lord Whitehead and the Zitmen. They played something Ian called industrial music, banging on hollowed-out washing machines, microwaves, etc. to pre-recorded rock music. Carrie had told Emma how bad they were. But she knew it was tough for Ian, because his father was the famous rock star Graham Perry, and naturally everyone compared Ian to his father.

"So, how should we go about this?" Emma asked nervously as they strode down the boardwalk, Katie clutching her hand tightly. She felt uncomfortable asking strangers for money, even if it was for a truly worthy cause.

"We show them our official COPE badges," Sam said, flashing the laminated card she'd been given the night before, "then we give them the rap, then we take the bucks."

"I don't know if it will be that easy," Carrie cautioned.

"Hey, how about if we start on High Street?" Sam suggested. "I saw this gorgeous guy on the front porch with his shirt off. . . ."

"Actually, I think we should split up," Carrie said. "We don't have a lot of time to collect, and if each of us goes alone, we'll be able to hit up three times the number of people."

"Such a practical girl," Sam said, pulling her red curls up into a ponytail. "So how about if *I* start on High Street, then?"

"I'll head up the hill past the dunes," Emma decided.

"Well, that leaves me with the streets behind the country club," Carrie said. "If we cover all of that, we'll have done our entire area."

"It won't be as much fun alone," Sam sighed.

"So console yourself with the shirtless guy," Carrie said with a chuckle.

"What's *console* mean?" Katie asked.

"To make someone feel better," Emma explained.

Katie looked over at Sam. "Do you feel bad, Sam?"

"I won't once I go meet that guy," Sam told her with a wink.

"Do you have a lot of boyfriends?" Katie asked Sam.

"Yep," Sam answered, putting her sunglasses back on.

"I want to have a lot of boyfriends, too," Katie decided.

"Good for you, you fox-of-the-future," Sam told the little girl. "Okay, I'm off. Call me later and tell me how it went, okay?"

Sam waved good-bye. Carrie took off, too, leaving Emma and Katie heading up the hill toward the dunes.

"Hello, I'm Emma Cresswell from COPE," Emma practiced as she and Katie walked along. "Hi there! I am Emma Cresswell!" she tried again in a perkier voice.

"You sound funny," Katie said, wrinkling her nose.

"You're right," Emma sighed. "I'll just have to wing it."

Altogether too soon they reached the first house they were going to try. It was a modern structure made of wood and glass with a wraparound deck. Emma took a deep breath. "Here goes," she said under her breath, and marched up to the front door. She lifted Katie up so that she could ring the bell.

"Yes?" A slender woman with short brown hair answered the door. She wore white shorts and held a tennis racquet in her hand.

"Hello," Emma said in what she hoped was a pleasant voice. "I'm Emma Cresswell, and I'm here representing COPE. COPE is—"

"Katie Hewitt!" the woman cried, bending down to the little girl. "I'm Jennifer Tolan's aunt! I remember you from last summer! And you've grown so much!"

"Is Jennifer here?" Katie asked excitedly.

"She's coming up next week," the woman said. "I'm sure you'll see her at the club." The woman stood up. "I'm Leslie Darrington," she said, reaching out to shake Emma's hand. "My niece, Jennifer, was up here last summer and she just fell in love with Katie! In fact, Jennifer's parents are friends of Jeff and Jane."

"I'm their au pair," Emma said.

"Right!" Leslie said, nodding. "I remember seeing you last summer. Come on in!"

Emma and Katie entered the cool front hallway, and Emma quickly explained about COPE and their fundraising drive.

"Well, sure I'll give you a donation," Leslie said. "Let me get my checkbook out." She rummaged through her purse, which sat on a small marble table under a mirror, and

40

quickly scribbled a check. "There," she said, handing it to Emma. "I hope that helps."

"Yes, thank you so much," Emma said, sliding the check into her pocket.

"Happy to help," Leslie said.

"Can Jennifer come and play when she gets here?" Katie asked.

"Sure thing!" Leslie agreed. "I'll have her call you, okay?"

"Okay!" Katie echoed happily, waving good-bye.

"She was nice," Katie said as she and Emma walked back to the street.

"You, young lady, are one great sales tool!" Emma said laughingly. She pulled the check out of her pocket. It was for one hundred dollars. Although to Emma this was a piddling amount of money, the people from COPE had told them that they probably wouldn't get donations of more than twenty dollars.

"Katie, we are off to a great start!" Emma said, squeezing the little girl's hand.

"Did I help?" Katie asked.

"Big time!" She felt so much better! It hadn't been nearly as hard as she'd expected it to be.

"Okay, here we go again," she said a couple of minutes later as they walked up a stone path toward a white clapboard house with light blue trim.

"This house is pretty," Katie decided.

"It looks a lot like yours," Emma observed as she knocked on the front door. A middle-aged man with thinning blond hair answered the door. "Yes?" he asked in a guarded voice.

"Hello," Emma began, "I'm Emma Cresswell—"

"If you're another friend of Sheila's, she's not here," he said curtly.

Emma was taken aback. She had no idea what he was talking about. "Uh, no, I'm not a friend of Sheila's," she answered.

"Well, you look like her friends," he growled, eyeing Emma's expensive designer outfit. "You all spend a small fortune on clothes."

"Look, I don't even know who Sheila is," Emma said stiffly.

"My daughter," the man informed her. "So if you're not here for Sheila, then what?"

Emma took a deep breath. This was not going to be easy. "I'm here for COPE," she began. "COPE is an organization that—"

"I know what COPE is," the man inter-rupted. "It's that crazy bunch of malcon-tents. There was an article in *The Breakers* about them last summer," he added, naming the island's only newspaper.

"They—I mean we are certainly not mal-contents," Emma said in her frostiest voice. "It just so happens that there are some very poor people on this island who lost the little they had during the hurricane, and—"

"Look, Irma—" the man cut in.

"Emma," Emma corrected him in a steely tone.

"Whatever," the man sniffed dismissively. "The deal is, you're here trying to get a handout for these people, am I right?"

"I certainly wouldn't refer to it as a hand-out," Emma began.

"I worked for every penny I ever made," the man interrupted Emma again, "and I expect the rest of the world to do likewise. Get it?"

"Got it," Emma replied. She looked him over coolly, in the supercilious tradition of her mother, the inimitable Kat. "Thank you so much for your valuable time," she added, her voice dripping false sincerity. Emma grabbed Katie's hand and turned on her heel.

"But he didn't give us any money!" Katie protested.

"And he's not likely to, either," Emma said, trying to put some distance between herself and the horribly rude man.

"But I thought people were supposed to give you money," Katie said.

"It's their choice," Emma explained. "They don't have to contribute if they don't want to."

Katie walked along in silence for a moment. "You could have my allowance," she finally said.

Emma smiled down at her. "You are a good person, Katie Hewitt."

Katie grinned back up at her. "You are a good person, too, Emma Cresswell."

Emma laughed. She couldn't stay upset at that rude man for very long with Katie by her side.

"Look up there," Katie said in a hushed voice, pointing to an old house at the very top of the hill. "That's the ghost house."

"Katie, there's no such thing as ghosts," Emma said.

"Yes there is," Katie replied. "Chloe told me," she added gravely, naming the five-year-old Templeton child whom Carrie took care of.

"Well, Chloe's wrong, honey," Emma said. "It's just a very old house. Probably no one even lives there anymore."

"But Chloe said real ghosts live there," Katie said, her eyes wide. "Scary ones. You can't touch a ghost, but it can do things to you, like make you get all bloody."

Emma shook her head. The workings of Katie's mind amazed her sometimes. "Sweetie, ghosts are just a made-up, pretend thing," she said soothingly. "Like a cartoon."

They walked farther up the hill, and to Emma's surprise she saw that someone had pushed open the shutter on one of the front windows. The shutter swung in the light breeze, emitting a creaking noise.

"A ghost!" Katie screamed, grabbing Emma around the waist and burying her head against Emma's stomach.

"No, honey, it's just the shutter. The people who live there must have opened it," Emma said.

"You said no one lived there!" Katie cried. "It must be a ghost!"

Emma knelt down and held Katie at arm's length. "I just guessed that no one lived there," she explained. "But apparently someone does. A real person, just like us."

"It might be a ghost," Katie said, her lower lip quivering.

"I'll tell you what," Emma said. "I'll prove to you that whoever lives there is just a normal person. We'll go try to get a donation at that house."

"No! We'll get all bloody!" Katie screamed.

"Katie, you know I love you and I'd never do anything to hurt you, right?" Emma asked the little girl.

Katie nodded, her eyes round with fright.

"Okay, then. We'll go up to that house and you'll see that there are no ghosts, and then you'll feel better."

"You promise there aren't ghosts?" Katie asked. She put one finger in her mouth, a gesture left over from her baby days.

"I promise," Emma said.

"Cross your heart and hope to die?" Katie asked.

"Cross my heart and hope to die," Emma

echoed. "Now, come on." She led Katie toward the house.

Emma had to admit that it really did look like something from a gothic horror novel. Weathered black shutters framed an odd assortment of windows, and the roof was dominated by what looked like a circular walkway. The front door was at least ten feet tall and painted jet black. Emma stared up at it. It really was creepy-looking. She stifled a shudder, lest she scare Katie.

"I think maybe we should leave now," Katie said in a small voice. "Sally wouldn't like it here." Sally was Katie's favorite doll, to whom Katie often ascribed her own point of view.

"I'm sure the people here are perfectly normal," Emma assured the little girl. She reached up for the brass knocker on the door, then pulled her hand back. The knocker was in the shape of a skull.

Hoping Katie wouldn't notice the strange decoration, Emma pounded directly on the door. Just then a bird cawed overhead, and both Katie and Emma jumped.

"You're scared, too!" Katie accused.

"No, of course I'm not," Emma said. She

hated lying. *You're letting your imagination get the best of you,* Emma chastised herself. *You're supposed to be the adult here!*

Slowly, the heavy door creaked open. Emma and Katie looked up . . . and up, at a very tall, very thin man with a gaunt face. He wore an old black tuxedo.

"Yeeeees?" the man asked in a low voice.

"Uh, hello," Emma said nervously. "I'm Emma Cresswell. I'm here with COPE." She handed him her laminated COPE card, which he looked at curiously. "COPE stands for Citizens of Positive Ethics," Emma continued.

"Are you a citizen of positive ethics?" the tall man asked.

"I . . . I try to be," Emma said.

"Well, I'm only a butler, so I can't help you," the man answered. He handed Emma back her card. Emma thought she saw a small smile playing at the corners of his mouth.

Of course, he's the butler, Emma thought to herself. *A tuxedoed butler answers our front door, too! Emma, you are really losing it!*

"May I speak with whomever lives here?" Emma said pleasantly.

"Some people live here, and some people die here," the butler growled in his hoarse, low voice. Emma almost jumped.

"Emma, I want to go *now*," Katie whispered frantically.

"It's okay, honey," Emma said soothingly.

"But I have to go to the bathroom first!" Katie whispered.

"Is there a bathroom she could use?" Emma asked the butler.

He pointed one cadaverous finger toward a door off the hall.

"Come with me," Katie said, wrapping her fingers tightly around Emma's hand. Emma went willingly. She didn't particularly want to be alone with the creepy butler, anyway.

The bathroom was painted completely black. A coffin-shaped box held black tissues. A painting of a witch with crazed, evil eyes hung over the sink.

"I don't like it here," Katie whispered as she sat on the black toilet.

"Me neither," Emma admitted. No point in pretending everything in this house was normal. Katie was too smart to be fooled.

"Can we leave now?" Katie asked while Emma helped her wash her hands in the black sink.

"Yes," Emma said. She reached for the hand towel, which was, of course, black. Then to her horror she noticed that red handprints marched over the towel, as if someone had pressed the towel to their bloody hand over and over again. *It's just a design,* Emma realized with a sigh of relief. *The handprints are part of the towel.* Quickly Emma stashed it behind her and grabbed some of the tissues for Katie to wipe her hands with.

"We are outta here," Emma said resolutely as she opened the bathroom door.

It was then that she heard the first scream.

FOUR

"I want to go home!" Katie wailed, grabbing on to Emma.

"It's . . . it's okay," Emma said in as soothing a voice as she could muster. *That was the most blood-curdling scream I've ever heard,* Emma thought. *But I can't let Katie know how scared I am.*

"Here's what we're going to do," Emma said firmly to Katie. "We're going to march straight to the front door and walk out of here."

Emma took Katie by the hand and they headed for the hall. The butler was nowhere to be seen.

"Faster," Katie urged.

"See? Everything's fine now," Emma assured her. She reached for the large brass doorknob on the oversized door.

"Noooooooooo!"

Emma stopped dead in her tracks when she heard the loud, moaning cry. It seemed to be coming from upstairs. For just a moment, Emma was so scared that she couldn't move at all. Then Katie began crying hysterically, and Emma came to her senses.

Just as they were halfway out the door, Emma heard someone come thundering down the long, curved stairway.

"All right! All right! I'll get some!"

Emma turned to look, half expecting to see some horrible monster. But there stood a young woman about Emma's age, wearing jeans and a New York Yankees T-shirt. The young woman stopped on the third step and stared at Emma, clearly surprised to see someone in the house.

"Hi!" she said, recovering quickly. "Can I help you?"

"Uh . . . uh . . ." Emma stammered.

The girl came the rest of the way down the stairs. "Where's Simon?" she asked, looking around the hall.

"Is he the butler?" Emma asked, finding her voice.

"I'm here, miss," the butler said, coming into the hall from a room to the left. "That was the delivery person at the back door. The groceries are here." He turned his huge head to Emma and Katie, then looked back at the young woman. "There are guests," he added.

"So I see," the girl said with a laugh. She walked toward Emma and Katie, who cowered behind Emma's legs. "I'm Darcy Laken," she said, stretching out her hand in a friendly fashion.

"Emma Cresswell," Emma said faintly, shaking Darcy's hand.

"Is she a witch?" Katie whispered from behind Emma.

Darcy laughed. "I wish I were. Think of all the cool things I could do."

Simon gave a low laugh, nodded his head slightly, and disappeared into another room.

"He's a bad man," Katie whimpered.

"No, he's a prankster, is what he is," Darcy said, shaking her head. "So, anyway, what can I do for you?"

Emma thought maybe she should just

make her excuses and leave. No matter how normal Darcy seemed, this was a seriously weird place. On the other hand, she didn't want to fuel Katie's fears, so she took a deep breath and made her pitch.

"Well," Emma began, "I'm here representing an organization called COPE, and we—"

"Noooooooooo!" came the horrible moan once again. Emma looked up the stairs, as did Darcy.

"Someone's hurt!" Emma cried. "What's going on up there?"

"Oh, it's just Molly," Darcy said breezily.

"Just Molly?" Emma repeated, completely outraged. "Someone is obviously in horrible pain up there! You had better tell me what's going on, or I'll go to the police!"

"She'll probably call the police on me sooner than you will if I don't get her some ice cream, which is why she's yelling," Darcy said calmly.

Emma eyed Darcy skeptically. "You're telling me someone is making that racket because she wants ice cream?"

"You got it," Darcy said cheerfully. "Come on into the kitchen with me. You can tell me about COPE while I dig into the chocolate ripple." She looked behind Emma and caught Katie's eye. "Would you like some, too?"

Katie nodded. "But don't let go of my hand," Katie told Emma.

Emma and Katie followed Darcy into a huge, immaculate, all-white kitchen. Darcy got the ice cream out of the freezer.

"If this Molly person just wants ice cream," Emma asked, still not convinced, "why is she moaning? It sounds like she's crying 'No!'"

"She's crying 'Now,'" Darcy explained, licking some ice cream off her finger. She looked at Emma. "Want some?"

Emma shook her head. She still wasn't certain that Darcy was telling her the truth. "Why can't Molly just get her own ice cream?"

Darcy handed a dish of ice cream to Katie, and Emma lifted her onto a high stool at the counter to eat it.

"Molly's in a wheelchair," Darcy said, getting out two spoons. "Look, let me run this upstairs to her before she starts up again, and then I'll come back and we can talk."

Darcy smiled at Katie and then walked swiftly out of the kitchen.

"Maybe she's a good witch, like in *The Wizard of Oz*," Katie said, her mouth full of ice cream.

"There's no such thing as witches," Emma said, even though at that moment she wasn't quite sure. She looked around the kitchen, relieved that it looked perfectly normal—until she noticed the fruit bowl on the table. Mixed in with the peaches and cherries was a human hand. She felt her heart jump.

"Hey, Katie," Emma said in a low voice, not wanting to alarm her charge, "why don't you finish up and we'll leave?"

"Maybe she'll give me more," Katie said, spooning some ice cream into her mouth. "I like Darcy," she added. "She has pretty hair."

"That's nice," Emma said. It amazed her that the child had been terrorized just five minutes earlier, and now she seemed completely at ease. *Now it's just me who's terrorized*, raced Emma's thoughts.

"Okay, no more howls from upstairs," Darcy said, coming back into the kitchen. She sat down at the counter. "So what's this about COPE? I've heard about them, but I don't really know what they do."

"Maybe you should explain about Molly before I explain about COPE," Emma said guardedly. She tried not to look over at the fruit bowl.

Darcy smiled. "Yeah, I guess this all must seem pretty weird to you. I'm so used to it I forget, and we pretty much never have visitors." Darcy noticed that Katie had finished her ice cream. "More?" she asked Katie.

Katie nodded.

"But Katie, we haven't had lunch yet," Emma reminded the little girl.

"Ice cream for lunch is good," Katie explained.

"She's right," Darcy laughed, getting the ice cream back out of the freezer and spooning a small portion into Katie's bowl. "Here's the deal," Darcy began. "I work here, taking care of Molly Mason."

"The girl who was yelling," Katie filled in.

"Right," Darcy said. "She's sixteen. She was in a car accident about a year and a half ago—a drunk driver hit her. Now she's a paraplegic. Her parents hired me to take care of her."

"That's so horrible," Emma said. Her mind immediately flashed on her own horrible experience the previous summer. A friend had been killed while driving drunk. Emma, Carrie, Sam, Kurt, Billy, and Sam's friend Danny had all been passengers in the car, and because their friend had drunk less than they had, they'd all thought he was okay to drive. But he hadn't been, and he'd been killed. Emma still felt horribly guilty that she hadn't stopped him from driving.

"It *is* terrible," Darcy agreed. "The guy who hit her went to jail, but he'll be out in a few months—which really sucks, if you ask me."

"It doesn't seem fair," Emma murmured.

"Because it isn't fair," Darcy said. "Anyway, my family lives up in Bangor, I needed a job to put myself through college—I'm going to be a freshman at the University of Maine in the fall—and so here I am."

Darcy took Katie's empty ice cream dish and headed for the dishwasher, which gave Emma a chance to study her.

Katie was right, Darcy really did have

terrific hair. Raven-black and absolutely straight, it reached past her waist. She had high cheekbones, an aquiline nose, and long-lashed, startlingly violet eyes. On the tall side, Darcy looked quite athletic.

"So, that's my story," Darcy said, walking back to the counter. "What's yours?"

Emma told Darcy all about COPE and their fundraising drive.

"Well, I can't ask Mr. and Ms. Mason because they're not on the island right now," Darcy said. "But I could make a small contribution." She got a leather purse from the counter and took out a ten-dollar bill. "Sorry it's not more," she said. "I'm on a really tight budget."

"This is fine. It's great of you to help," Emma assured her.

Darcy looked at Emma with curiosity. "So, what's the deal with you, anyway? Is this little cutie your sister?"

"This is Katie Hewitt. I'm her au pair," Emma said, stroking Katie's hair.

Darcy laughed. "Ah, a hired hand just like me!" Then she glanced at Emma's expensive designer outfit and raised her eyebrows. "Babysitting pays well, huh?"

"I'm not in it for the money," Emma said stiffly. *Oh, listen to me*, she thought disgustedly. *If I don't sound like a prissy rich girl* . . .

"What *are* you in it for, then?" Darcy asked.

"For . . . for . . ." Emma stammered. Why *was* she an au pair? "You're extremely outspoken," Emma said defensively.

"That's true," Darcy agreed. "Usually I get called much worse." She lifted her knees up to her chin and put her arms around them. "Anyway, I wasn't judging you. I really can't stand judgmental people. I'm just curious."

Emma pushed her blond hair behind one ear. "I'm trying to find some answers in my life," she said simply.

"Sounds good to me," Darcy agreed reasonably.

"Do you think that girl upstairs ate all her ice cream?" Katie asked.

"Why don't we go ask her?" Darcy said, getting up. "She doesn't get a lot of visitors."

"Wait a minute," Emma said. "Look, you seem . . . well, perfectly normal, but this house doesn't." Emma's eyes strayed significantly to the human hand in the fruit bowl.

"It's a hoot, isn't it?" Darcy said, following Emma's gaze.

"A hoot? The skull-shaped door knocker? The bloody handprints on the towels in the bathroom? Shall I go on?"

"I got scared," Katie said gravely.

"I'm sorry you got scared," Darcy said. "You'd have to know the Masons to understand. They're . . . well, they're different. You see, this house has been in their family for generations, and it looks so spooky to begin with that they just decided to decorate it spooky."

"I suggest they stay away from interior decorating as a career choice," Emma deadpanned. Darcy laughed.

Emma looked at the fruit bowl again. "You mean that isn't really a—"

"It's plastic, honest," Darcy assured her. "Come on, I'll take you up to meet Molly."

Darcy led the way up the long, winding stairway. "Molly! We have visitors!" Darcy called ahead of her.

"No!" a voice shouted. "I don't want to see anyone!"

They turned into a room all decorated in

pink and white, with trophies lining a shelf along the wall. A teenage girl with curly brown hair sat in a wheelchair in the middle of the room.

"I said no visitors!" the girl in the wheelchair seethed through clenched teeth.

"Molly, this is Emma Cresswell and Katie Hewitt. And this is Molly Mason," Darcy said.

"Charmed," Molly said, her voice dripping sarcasm.

"Emma is collecting money for the poor people whose homes got destroyed by the hurricane," Darcy told Molly. "Want to make a contribution?"

"No," Molly said, "and I don't want company, either. Do you have a hearing problem?"

Darcy leaned against Molly's desk, seemingly unfazed by Molly's attitude.

"Oh, come on, Mol," Darcy chided her, "lighten up. Want to go outside on the widow's walk? We could all talk there. It's beautiful out."

"What's a widow's walk?" Katie whispered to Emma.

"It's that walkway outside, all around the

top floor of the house," Darcy explained, hearing Katie's question. "It was called a widow's walk because women would watch from there to see if their husbands came home from the sea. I guess sometimes they didn't."

Katie walked shyly up to Molly. "Why are you in that chair?"

"Because I can't walk," Molly snapped.

"Ever?" Katie asked.

Molly gave Darcy a look of disgust. "Excuse me, but this is not show-and-tell," she answered Katie, and to Darcy she added, "For once couldn't you do what I tell you to do?"

"Which is?" Darcy asked.

"Leave, and take them with you," Molly said bluntly.

"Okay," Darcy said easily, getting up from the desk. "See you later."

Emma and Katie followed Darcy back downstairs to the main hall.

"She's very angry," Emma ventured.

"Wouldn't you be?" Darcy asked, pausing on the bottom step.

"I suppose I would," Emma allowed, "but she still shouldn't treat you so badly."

"She's having a tough day," Darcy said. "Did you notice those trophies on her wall? She won those in equestrian shows—that's horseback riding," she added for Katie's benefit. "Today is the annual Sunset Country Club Equestrian Competition. Molly won it two years ago."

"Couldn't she still ride?" Emma asked.

"The doctors say it's a long shot but I think she could," Darcy said. "But she won't even go out in public if she can help it."

"Well, we'd better be going," Emma said, taking Katie's hand. "Thanks for the contribution to COPE."

"And the ice cream," Katie added.

"Anytime," Darcy said. For a moment she looked down at the highly polished black marble floor. When she looked at Emma again, her expression seemed shyer. "You know, no one much comes to see Molly, and I don't really know any kids on the island. I mean, if you ever want to stop by again, well, I'd really like it."

"What happened to Molly's friends?" Emma asked with curiosity. "Surely she still has friends."

"Not really," Darcy said with a shrug. "I

guess she didn't have that many close friends to begin with, and the few she had she's chased away." Darcy twisted a few strands of hair contemplatively. "You'd think they'd understand, wouldn't you? You'd think they'd stand by her and help her work through her anger. But no one has."

"Except you," Emma pointed out.

"Like I said, I'm a hired hand," Darcy said. She looked upstairs. "But the truth is, I really like Molly. You'd like her, too, if you ever have a chance to get to know her."

"Say, I have an idea," Emma said. "To-morrow I'm supposed to meet two friends of mine at the country club around two o'clock. They're au pairs, too—so we'll all have our kids with us. Why don't you and Molly meet us there?"

"That's a great idea!" Darcy said, her face lighting up. "I'll really have to work on Molly, though."

"Well, try," Emma said. "We'll meet by the main pool."

Darcy knelt down to Katie. "Will you be there?"

"Yep, I swim," Katie said proudly. "Kurt taught me."

"Kurt?" Darcy said. "Oh, right, the swimming instructor. I've seen him at the club a few times. He's gorgeous."

"He's my boyfriend," Katie said. She looked up at Emma. "Really, he's Emma's boyfriend," she admitted.

"Lucky you," Darcy told Emma, standing up.

"So, I hope we'll see you tomorrow," Emma said as Darcy opened the huge front door.

"Me, too," Darcy agreed.

Emma stepped outside and looked up at the skull-shaped doorknocker. "Extremely bizarre," she commented.

Darcy laughed. "What did you think of the doorbell?" she asked.

Emma looked puzzled, so Darcy leaned past her and pressed the bell. The same blood-curdling scream Emma had heard before echoed throughout the hallway.

Emma's eyes widened for a moment. Then it hit her. "The door bell—it screams?"

Darcy nodded. "Didn't you hear it when the delivery person from the grocery store came to the back door?"

All Emma could do was shake her head. "Like I said, bizarre."

Darcy smiled. "Wait till you meet Molly's parents. Then you'll really know what bizarre is."

Emma caught a glimpse of Simon, the butler, as he crossed silently through the hall. "He's not exactly your run-of-the-mill butler, either," she whispered.

"Frustrated actor," Darcy whispered back. "He watches reruns of *The Addams Family* on TV every afternoon." A startled look came to Darcy's face. "Uh-oh, Molly needs me. I'd better run. See you tomorrow!"

Emma said good-bye. She took Katie's hand and they started down the walk back to the street. *Now, how did Darcy know that Molly needed her?* Emma wondered. She hadn't heard Molly call out. She hadn't heard anything at all.

"I like her," Katie said. "She's a good witch."

"I told you, honey, there's no such thing as witches," Emma said.

But even as she said it, she wasn't *entirely* sure it was the truth.

FIVE

"That place sounds mondo bizarro," Sam said, pulling suntan lotion out of her beach-bag.

It was the next afternoon, and Emma, Carrie, and Sam had met at the club as planned. Their various charges were all off in the pool, and the girls were alone. Emma had just finished telling them about her experience at the Masons' house.

"A skull for a doorknocker?" Carrie asked. "A human hand in the fruit bowl?"

Emma laughed. "I have to admit, I was scared myself for a while. But Darcy is perfectly normal. Anyway, you'll see—if she was able to talk Molly into coming, they should be here any minute."

"Can you imagine how awful it would be to be stuck in a wheelchair?" Carrie asked.

"I'd rather be dead," Sam announced, spreading suntan lotion on her legs.

"You don't mean that," Emma said, sitting up to straighten the towel she was lying on.

"I do mean it," Sam said. "I'm a dancer. I couldn't stand it."

"Well, as my mom always says," Carrie began, "you can't necessarily control the hand you're dealt, but you *can* control how you play it."

"*Carrie's Little Instruction Book*, lesson three hundred and sixty-one," Sam intoned.

Carrie gave Sam a level look. "All I have to say is, you're lucky nothing really terrible has happened to you in your life."

"Hey, how's it going?" a deep male voice said.

Emma smiled up at Kurt, who was looking tanned, fit, and gorgeous in blue-and-white surfer jams. "My favorite lifeguard," she greeted him.

"Your favorite lifeguard has to stay an extra hour today, to give Alexandra Pope a private swimming lesson," Kurt said, sitting on the edge of Emma's lounge chair. Alexandra Pope was the thirteen-year-old girl whom Lorell allegedly was watching for the summer. In actuality, Alexandra's wealthy parents were friends of Lorell's even wealthier parents, and Lorell didn't have to do any work at all.

"Why can't she take lessons with the other kids?" Sam asked Kurt.

"She's gotten even chubbier this summer, and she's real self-conscious about being around the other kids," Kurt explained.

"That's a shame," Emma said. "It must be so hard on her."

"Yeah, kids can be really cruel," Sam said. "I used to get called stork, bird legs—all the usual geeky tall-girl names."

"No one calls you names anymore," Carrie pointed out.

"Yesterday's geek can be today's hot mama, and I am living proof," Sam opined, adjusting her chair.

"So listen," Kurt told Emma, "my car is out of the shop. After Alexandra's lesson I'll run home and change, then pick you up about nine for Howie's party, okay?"

"Okay," Emma agreed. She turned to Carrie and Sam. "Are you two going?"

"I have to stay with Chloe and Ian tonight," Carrie said with a sigh.

"I'll be there with Pres," Sam said.

"Great. So we'll meet up at the party," Emma said.

Kurt leaned over and kissed Emma on the neck. "Wear something short," he whispered in her ear.

"Wear something tight," she whispered back, amazed at her own audacity.

Kurt laughed and headed back to the pool.

"Emma Cresswell, I heard that," Sam said with a laugh. "All I have to say is, you have come *so* far!"

Emma smiled. Sam was right. The summer before, she never would have had the nerve to banter with Kurt like that. Emma watched Kurt walk over to some little kids at the junior pool. *Yum,* she thought mischievously, *and he's all mine.* She thought about what a fabulous time they were going to have that night. Then she remembered that she'd have to tell Kurt about her mother's engagement party. Thinking about the party soured her mood, and she sat for a while stewing about her mother and the creep she was planning to marry.

"Hi there!" Darcy said, striding over to Emma's lounge chair and interrupting her train of thought. "Sorry I'm late. I was trying to talk Molly into coming, but as you can see, I didn't succeed."

"Well, I'm glad you came anyway," Emma said, shielding her eyes from the sun so she could look up at Darcy. "This is Carrie Alden, and the redhead in the world's teeniest bikini over there is Sam Bridges," she said. "And this is Darcy Laken. Darcy, I've told Carrie and Sam all about you."

"Nice to meet you," Carrie said. "Pull up a chair."

"I really did work on Molly," Darcy continued, dragging another lounge chair close to the girls.

"Hey, she can't stay cooped up in that haunted house forever," Sam said.

"She can if she wants to," Darcy said, shrugging.

"She's crazy, if you ask me," Sam said bluntly.

"Hey, it's her legs that got messed up, not her mind," Darcy told Sam.

"I guess she thinks people will stare at her," Carrie said softly.

"Correction," Darcy said. "She *knows* people will stare at her. The few times we've gone out in public, people look at her like she's subhuman. A lot of people treat her as though she were retarded."

"Well, the kind of people who are stupid enough to do that are the kind of people she doesn't need," Sam said vehemently.

"Easy for you to say," Darcy said mildly. "You're not the one who has to go through it."

"No, I guess not," Sam said. She shot Emma a significant look that obviously meant *your new friend is obnoxious*. Emma ignored her.

"It's really gorgeous out," Darcy said, standing up to unzip her white cotton shorts. She pulled off her turquoise T-shirt and stuffed it into her beachbag with the shorts.

"Cute bathing suit," Emma said, eyeing Darcy's simple one-piece red suit with high-cut legs and black piping. Emma noticed that Darcy's build was muscular and athletic. And while she certainly didn't fit into the current petit mode of perfection featured in the pages of the fashion magazines,

Darcy looked terrific and seemed completely comfortable in her own skin.

"Hey, anyone want to go for a swim?" Sam asked, sitting up and slipping her sunglasses into her beachbag. "I think I'd better go do something about the monsters. They're in the deep end talking to two college guys. They probably told them they're eighteen," she said with a groan.

"Who are the monsters?" Darcy asked, getting up.

Sam began to explain about Becky and Allie Jacobs, the girls she was caring for, as she and Darcy walked away.

"I like her," Carrie decided. "She's very direct."

"I like her, too," Emma said, "although I'm not sure Sam does."

"No, I think she does. They seem to be having a good conversation," Carrie pointed out. "You'd expect them to clash a little, though, since Sam's pretty direct herself. Did you ever notice how often people dislike a quality in other people that they have themselves?"

Emma laughed. "Carrie, you were in the right line when God handed out brains."

"And looks. And personality. And modesty!" Carrie added with mock innocence.

"Whew! The water's great!" Darcy said as she padded back over to the girls a few minutes later and picked up her towel.

"Where did you learn to dive like that?" Carrie asked her.

"I have three older brothers," Darcy said with a grin. "Living in my house, I pretty much had to learn to play any sport ever invented."

Just then a dripping Sam arrived. "Three older brothers?" she echoed, wiggling her eyebrows. She began to towel-dry her wet hair. *"Cute* older brothers?"

"So I've been told," Darcy said. "You guys will have to meet them sometime." She looked at her watch. "I'm going to have to run. Simon is watching Molly, but she hates it when I'm gone for any length of time."

"Sounds like being an au pair," Sam said. "Except our kids are younger."

"Well, Molly is my job, but she's also my friend," Darcy said.

"Hey, I didn't mean—" Sam began.

"I know you didn't," Darcy said, hoisting

her beachbag over her shoulder. "Listen, thanks again for the invite. I had fun."

"Hey, do you want to go to a party tonight?" Sam asked Darcy. "There's going to be a real blowout at our friend's house."

"I'd love to, but I know I'd never convince Molly to come to a party," Darcy said with a shrug.

"Well, how about lunch tomorrow, then?" Emma asked, sitting up. "The three of us have already made plans to meet at the Play Café about one o'clock. You think you could get Molly out for lunch?"

"It's a good place to start," Darcy said. "I'll give it a try." She pulled her sunglasses out of her bag. "So with any luck, Molly and I will see you guys tomorrow. Bye!"

"I really like her," Sam said as they watched Darcy walk away.

"Really?" Emma asked. "I wasn't sure you did."

"Well, I didn't at first," Sam admitted. "But you should have heard her with Becky just now. Just as I suspected, Becky and Allie told those guys they were eighteen instead of thirteen," she said ruefully. "So Darcy told Becky that the guy she was talking to—see that guy down there with the curly black hair? Him." Sam pointed him out. "Well, Darcy told Becky that guy had gotten thrown out of college for stealing. So Becky went and asked the guy and he said no, but the other guy laughed and said, 'You are such a liar, Johnson!'"

"How did Darcy know that?" Carrie asked. "Does she know him?"

"Nope," Sam said. "Those guys go to Penn State. I asked Darcy how she knew, and she said it was a lucky guess."

"That's pretty strange," Carrie said. "Do you think she has ESP or something?"

"I think she's a witch," Sam said whimsically, settling down on her lounge chair, "and she fits right in with that spook house she lives in. Anyway, I make a point never to get on the bad side of a witch." Sam closed her eyes. "Wake me if one of the monsters drowns."

Carrie chuckled and got a book out of her bag, but Emma wasn't laughing. No matter how normal Darcy Laken looked, there was definitely something strange about the girl.

SIX

"You look great," Kurt told Emma as he took her into his arms. They had arrived at Howie Lawrence's house just in time to catch the beginning of a Michael Bolton ballad coming through the speakers.

"Thanks," Emma said demurely, lacing her fingers behind Kurt's neck. She'd worn a plain, short white linen shift that she knew Kurt liked. "You're looking pretty tasty yourself," she added with a grin. Kurt had on faded jeans and a soft, well-worn denim shirt. A red bandana was tied around his head.

She moved closer to him until she could feel the cotton of his shirt under her cheek. "Mmm, this feels terrific," she whispered in his ear.

"Hi, guys, glad you could make it!" Howie said, coming up beside them and giving Emma a friendly hug.

"Great party," Kurt told him. "There must be a hundred people in here!"

"I aim to please," Howie said with a grin. He pushed his glasses farther up his nose— they always seemed to be slipping down. "Have you seen Carrie?"

Howie had a huge crush on Carrie, Emma knew, which unfortunately for Howie wasn't reciprocated. "She had to babysit," Emma said.

Howie's face fell. "Maybe she's coming later?" he asked hopefully. "I mean, we'll be partying till dawn."

"I don't think so, Howie," Emma said. "Sorry."

"Well, tell her I was asking about her, okay?"

"Sure," Emma said with a kind smile.

"That guy has a great attitude," Kurt said after Howie had walked away.

"Mooning over a girl who isn't interested in him?" Emma asked, slipping easily back into Kurt's arms.

"No, I mean never giving up," Kurt said,

encircling Emma's tiny waist. "He's crazy about that girl, and he doesn't care who knows it."

Emma lifted her head from Kurt's shoulder and looked at him. "Are you that crazy about me?"

"Fishing for compliments, eh?" Kurt asked with a grin.

"Yes," Emma answered, grinning back.

"Crazier," Kurt said. "Insane. I'm completely nuts about you." He pulled her closer. "How's that?"

"Perfect," Emma sighed.

"Ah, young love, or is it young lust?" Sam crowed, coming up next to Kurt and Emma. She and Pres were holding hands.

"Try it, you might like it," Kurt told Sam.

Sam looked at Pres. "I suggest we go for the lust part. How about you?"

"Girl, lucky for you I know you're not half as tough as you talk," Pres told Sam in his easy Tennessee drawl. He put his arms around her and pulled her close to dance. Sam waved once at Emma, then snuggled closer to Pres and moved to the music.

Emma closed her eyes and swayed in Kurt's arms. She could feel the heat of his body right through his clothes. The thought that she was responsible for the rise in temperature excited her.

"Em, I really want to be alone with you," Kurt whispered in her ear.

"Me, too," she whispered back.

Silently Kurt took her hand and led her through the crowd to the deck. Then they walked down the redwood steps that led to the beach.

For a moment, Kurt just stared at Emma in the moonlight. Then he put his arms around her and kissed her softly. He kissed her again, harder this time, and she kissed him back until she felt breathless.

"God, Emma, I've missed this," Kurt breathed in her ear. "I've missed *you*. It seems like we never have enough time to be alone together."

"We're alone now," Emma whispered. She laced her fingers around his neck and kissed him again.

Kurt put his hands around Emma's waist and lifted her off the sand. His lips still on hers, he moved forward until Emma's back was pressed against one of the redwood pillars that supported the deck above. She could feel every part of him, every muscle in his body. It was the most wonderful feeling in the world—dizzy, out of control.

"I love you, Emma," Kurt whispered into her hair. "I want you so much."

"Me, too," Emma admitted. At that moment, all her wise, mature ideas about waiting to make love until the time was right seemed ridiculous. All she cared about was being as close to Kurt as she possibly could.

"Let's go down by the dunes," Kurt said huskily, grabbing Emma's hand.

He wants us to go make love right now, Emma thought wildly, *right out on the beach!*

"But . . . but . . ." she stammered.

"You don't have to worry," Kurt said, bending to kiss her again. "I brought condoms."

Emma moved away a bit. "Were you that sure I'd say yes?"

"I just hoped, that's all," Kurt said, reaching out to stroke Emma's hair.

Emma's emotions were in a complete jumble. She wanted to be with Kurt, but not like this, not on a beach where anyone might catch them. She had waited so long for this moment that she wanted it to be special when it finally happened. On the other hand, here was the guy she loved with all her heart holding out his hand to her, and her whole body yearned for him.

"No, Kurt, not like this," Emma finally said. "I want . . . I want us to be alone, in a bed, someplace beautiful."

Kurt's hand dropped to his side. "How are we going to arrange that?"

"You could do it," Emma coaxed.

"Oh, Em." Kurt sighed. "It can't be on the island, because if we rented a hotel room here, everyone would know inside of an hour. Besides, I can't afford the prices on this island. Do you really think the No-Tell Motel off the highway would be more romantic than the dunes?"

Emma reached up and smoothed Kurt's hair. "No, not someplace sleazy like that. Some place like the Sentry," she said softly.

"The Sentry?" Kurt repeated. The Sentry was a four-star hotel on the mainland, just a ferry ride away from Sunset Island. "Do you have any idea what one night at the Sentry costs? It's probably two hundred dollars!"

"I'll pay for it," Emma said easily.

"No, you won't," Kurt answered in a steely voice.

"But what difference does it make?" Emma asked, "as long as we're together?"

Kurt stared at Emma a moment and didn't answer. "Come on," he finally said, "let's take a walk. I need to cool off."

They both took off their shoes, and hand in hand they walked across the sand. The full moon cast a silvery light on their faces.

"Don't you think it bothers me not to be able to afford to take you someplace nice?" Kurt asked Emma in a low voice.

"Yes, I understand," Emma said, "but it doesn't matter to me. The money doesn't mean anything."

"We're not talking about you, we're talking about me!" Kurt shot back. Then he sighed again. "I love you, Emma, but you just don't get it. You can't understand how I feel."

"Yes, I can!" Emma protested.

"No, you can't," Kurt said. "Just getting my junky car repaired wrecked my budget, but I have to have a car. But that means I don't have enough money for my tuition this fall, and it doesn't look like I'm going to be able to make it up, even if I work extra for what's left of the summer."

Emma stopped walking and turned to Kurt. "Why didn't you tell me? That's what you're really worried about!"

"What good would it do?" Kurt asked. "It's my problem."

"When people love each other, they share their problems!" Emma cried. "Besides, I can loan you the money for your tuition."

"Which is exactly why I didn't tell you," Kurt snapped. Then he seemed to realize how mean he sounded. "I'm sorry," he said, taking a deep breath. "I know you mean well, but I can't take your money."

Kurt studied the moon's reflection in the water. "You're used to living like a rich person," he said softly. "You can't imagine anything else. But I bet something as small as your earrings"—he touched the diamond studs in Emma's earlobes—"could probably have paid my sister's community-college tuition, with money left over." He ran his hand through his hair. "It doesn't seem right, does it?"

"I guess it doesn't," Emma answered.

Kurt gazed at the expensive houses beyond the dunes. "And those houses—I noticed that the people who own the one next to the Lawrences' use it maybe one weekend a month. All that stuff in there, and they hardly use it. Meanwhile, people on this island are homeless." He looked back at Emma. "Can you make any sense out of that?"

"But there have always been rich people and poor people," Emma said, struggling with her own thoughts. "This is America. Everything isn't equal."

"It sure isn't," Kurt said bitterly. He gave Emma a strange look. "Listen, I need to be alone for a while. I'm going to take a walk down the beach."

"By yourself?" Emma said. She felt as though she was about to cry. How could everything have changed so suddenly? Why did she and Kurt always seem to end up fighting about money?

"Oh, Em, it's not you, it's me," Kurt said, putting his arms around her and kissing her softly. "I'll meet you back at Howie's later."

"No," Emma said, pulling away. "If you go, don't bother to come back to find me." A voice inside Emma cried, *That isn't what you mean at all! Just tell him that you're hurt!*

"If that's how you want it," Kurt said. He sounded more tired than angry. "For what it's worth, I'm sorry," he added, then walked off down the beach.

I can't believe he left me here by myself! Emma thought. One part of her wanted to call out to him, but another part knew she should let him be. *Why does love have to be so damned complicated?*

Emma bit her lower lip, willing herself not to cry. She turned around to head back to the party. Lost in thought, she stared at her footprints in the sand. *It feels like he's punishing me for being rich*, she thought desolately.

When she got back to the party, it was in full swing and the noise was deafening.

"Hey, you are not looking like a party animal," Sam yelled over the music when she saw Emma.

"I don't want to talk about it," Emma said. "Can I have a ride home?"

Sam's eyebrows shot up. "Where's Kurt?" Then the look on Emma's face registered. "Oh, I guess that's what you don't want to talk about." She put her hand on Emma's arm. "It's okay, Em. You can talk when you're ready, okay?"

Emma just nodded, too choked up to speak.

"You ready, darlin'?" Pres said, coming up next to Sam.

Sam looked at Emma. "We were just going to leave, anyway. Come on."

"Thanks," Emma said gratefully. She didn't want to see anyone or talk to anyone, so she made a beeline for the front door with her head down. But a high-pitched laugh and a glint of a diamond tennis bracelet caught her eye just as she reached the door. Then she heard Diana De Witt's unmistakeable voice.

"Really, Austin, you can't see through this dress unless I get it *wet!*"

Emma looked up just in time to see Diana moving into the arms of her mother's fiancé, Austin Payne. She looked away quickly, hoping they hadn't seen her. She pushed out the front door and ran out to Pres's car.

Pres and Sam drove Emma back to the Hewitts' in silence, since it was obvious she didn't want to talk.

"I'll call you," Sam said quietly when Emma got out of the car.

"Thanks," Emma managed, shutting the car door.

She ran upstairs and angrily tore off her clothes, then got into bed and pulled the covers over her head.

I hate my life, was her final thought as she fell into a deep and troubled sleep.

In her nightmare, a naked Diana and an equally naked Kurt were kissing on a waterbed. Then Kurt's face turned into Austin's, and Diana started laughing, a mad cackle that turned into an incessant ring. Finally Emma opened her eyes, realizing that the telephone was really ringing.

She squinted at the luminous hands of the clock by her bed as she threw off the covers. It was five o'clock in the morning!

"Hello?" she answered groggily when she reached the phone.

"Emma? It's me," came Kurt's voice through the receiver.

"Are you crazy?" Emma whispered hoarsely. "It's not even dawn!"

"Emma! Please listen!" Kurt cried. "I'm in jail."

That woke Emma up instantly. "You're *where?*"

"In jail," Kurt repeated. He sounded scared out of his mind. "I've been arrested for armed robbery."

SEVEN

"What?" she cried into the phone. "You're *where?*"

"In jail," Kurt repeated in a desperate voice. "You know the house next door to the Lawrences' that we walked by last night? Well, somebody robbed them. A lot of valuable jewelry was taken," he continued.

"Oh, God, that's horrible!" Emma cried. "But why do they think it was you?"

"Someone gave the cops a description of the robber, and they described me," he said grimly, "right down to the clothes I was wearing last night."

"How . . . how can that be?" Emma's voice faltered.

"Emma! I didn't do it!" Kurt cried. "I don't know how it can be!"

"I believe you! Of course I believe you!" Emma insisted.

"Look, please, you've got to get me out of here," Kurt said in a low voice.

What can I do? she thought. *Would Jane help?* Emma's employer *was* a lawyer, after all.

"Emma? Come on! This is my one phone call! Emma?" Kurt asked, a note of near-panic in his voice.

"Listen, Kurt," Emma replied, "I'm going to wake Jane and tell her what happened. She'll know what to do. Where exactly are you?"

"In the holding tank at the police station," Kurt replied. "There's some drunk guy in here who's trying to throw up on me. My arraignment, whatever that means, is set for nine this morning," he added grimly.

"I'm going to get Jane now," Emma assured Kurt. "Don't worry. We'll be right down."

"Thanks," Kurt said gratefully.

Emma hung up the phone. *Did I really have that conversation, or am I still in the middle of that nightmare?* she wondered.

Emma pulled on her robe, intending to head over to Jane and Jeff Hewitt's bedroom. But before she even opened her bedroom door, she heard a knock on it. Jane Hewitt, dressed in her pajamas, poked her head inside.

"Everything okay?" Jane asked in a worried tone. "I heard the phone ring before."

Emma sat down on her bed. "No, everything's not okay. Kurt's been arrested," she said.

"Kurt?" Jane repeated in a shocked voice. "What happened?"

Emma told Jane everything that Kurt had told her about his arrest, including the fact that his arraignment was scheduled for nine, less than four hours away.

"What's an arraignment?" Emma asked.

"It's when a defendant is brought before a judge, formally told what he's been arrested for, and bail is usually set," Jane said.

"You mean I can bail him out of jail?" Emma queried.

"Yep," Jane said. She sat down on the bed next to Emma. "Listen, Emma, I know Kurt, and if he says he didn't do this, he didn't do it."

Emma smiled at her gratefully.

"I'll tell you what we need to do," Jane continued. "The two of us should go down to the police station. I'm licensed to practice law in Maine, and while criminal law isn't my specialty—I haven't done an arraignment since right after law school—I think I could handle it."

"That'd be great! I'll post bail!" Emma nearly shouted with joy.

"Okay, let's put some clothes on, and I'll meet you downstairs," Jane said, turning to the door. "Meet you in fifteen minutes."

Emma pulled on a pair of cotton pants and an oversized sweatshirt, and quickly washed her face and brushed her hair. By the time she got downstairs, Jane was already waiting for her.

They drove to the police station in silence. After they parked the Hewitts' car in the nearly empty lot, they walked inside, Jane carrying a small briefcase.

"Fortunately," Jane said to Emma as they hurried inside, "most of the cops probably know Kurt personally. I wouldn't be surprised if Judge Easton knows him, too. That'll help at the bail hearing."

Inside the police station, the desk officer had Jane fill out some forms indicating she was going to represent Kurt at that morning's arraignment. Then, after Jane told her that Emma was her assistant, the desk officer patted both Jane and Emma down for weapons before leading the two of them to the dank cell in which Kurt was being held.

"Ackerman!" the desk officer yelled as they approached. "Counsel here to see you."

Kurt nearly jumped for joy when he saw Jane and Emma.

"God, I've never been so glad to see anyone in my life," he said, putting his arms around Emma.

Emma held Kurt close. "It's going to be fine now," she assured him. She loved him so much! Their earlier fight seemed like such a stupid waste of time.

Kurt pulled away from Emma and looked at Jane. "Can you help get me out of here?" he asked. "I don't know how this could have happened! I didn't do it!"

"Kurt, calm down," Jane said in a very businesslike voice. "I'm going to level with you. You are in a lot of trouble. The good news is you are being charged for burglary, not armed robbery. There was some confusion about the pocket knife you were carrying. But burglary at least is not nearly as serious as armed robbery. Eventually, you are going to get to tell your side of the story. But this morning, the judge isn't going to care whether you did it or not. He's only going to tell you officially what you're being charged with, and then set your bail."

"But I didn't do it!" Kurt repeated in a ragged voice. "Doesn't anybody care about that? I'm totally innocent! They should drop all the charges!"

"They're not dropping the charges today," Jane said softly. "So let's talk about bail. Emma has agreed to post it for you."

Jane took out a yellow legal pad, and Emma watched her ask Kurt a series of questions about his job, his family, and his school record, carefully noting each answer.

"This stuff is for the bail hearing," she explained. "They're going to want to see that you're not likely to jump bail and leave the island. By the way, do you know Judge Easton?"

"He was my Little League coach!" Kurt exclaimed.

"How'd you get along with him?" Jane asked.

"Great, until I struck out twice in the big game against Old Orchard Beach." Kurt tried to smile.

"Well, we'll see if he still holds it against you." Jane patted Kurt's shoulder. "We'll see you in court in a few hours."

Kurt and Emma quickly embraced, and then Jane and Emma left.

Could he possibly have done it? Emma found herself wondering. *No way!* But she couldn't erase a tiny, niggling doubt in the back of her mind. *He's always been unhappy about being so poor—and burglary is one way to get rich quick. But no, I know Kurt better than that. He is the most moral, most ethical person I know. He'd sooner starve to death than steal from someone.*

Jane and Emma went out to breakfast to pass the time, although neither of them found they could eat anything. Jane drank three cups of coffee and Emma managed to swallow a cup of tea. *How can I eat*, she thought, *while Kurt is stuck in jail, scared out of his mind?*

Nearly three hours later, Jane sat at the

defense table in the small Sunset Island courtroom, while Emma sat in the front of the tiny spectator area. A young lawyer from the district attorney's office sat at the prosecution table. A bailiff entered and shouted "All rise!" Judge Easton strode in. Emma could see that under his judicial robes he wore a plain sweatshirt and trousers.

"Be seated," Judge Easton said in a strong Maine accent. "Just one case on today's docket. Arraignment and bail hearing, case number three-four-eight-three-seven-nine. People versus Kurt Ackerman. Please bring in the defendant."

The bailiff went to a side room and re-emerged with Kurt. Kurt was wearing a jail-issue orange coverall. *He looks like a criminal!* Emma thought, shocked. The bailiff escorted Kurt to the table where Jane was waiting.

Reading from a folder in front of him, Judge Easton announced that Kurt had been charged with a single count of burglary, and cited the section of the Maine penal code Kurt was charged with violating. "How do you plead?" the judge concluded.

Jane stood and spoke for Kurt. "The defendant enters a plea of not guilty," she said in a clear voice.

"Bail portion of the hearing," Judge Easton said, looking at both the prosecutor and Jane. "Does the state have anything to say before I set bail?"

The district attorney rose. "The people recommend setting bail at fifty thousand dollars to prevent the possibility of flight by the defendant."

"Counsel?" Judge Easton asked, looking at Jane.

Jane stood and argued that Kurt's family were longtime residents of the Sunset Island community, that Kurt held two jobs on the island, and that he was a good student at the University of Maine. She requested that Kurt be released on his own recognizance, without having to post any money.

Judge Easton considered all this in silence, and then spoke. "I've known the defendant for many years. He's not going to run away. Nonetheless, this is a serious crime you're charged with, Kurt. I'm setting your bail at five thousand dollars. And Kurt?"

Kurt spoke for the first time. "Yes, Your Honor?"

"Don't you strike out on me again. You jump bail, we're going to find you, lock you up, and throw away the key. Trial is set for October twenty-third. Court adjourned!"

An hour later, Kurt was free. Jane had driven them all back to the Hewitts' house, and then politely excused herself so that Kurt and Emma could talk alone. Kurt and Emma sat on the back porch and drank steaming-hot mugs of coffee—a first for Emma, who always drank tea. But it had been a long night for them both.

Kurt looked directly at Emma with red-rimmed eyes. "Thanks. For everything," he said softly.

"You don't need to thank me," Emma answered.

"It seems pretty funny, doesn't it?" Kurt said. "I was ragging on you for wanting to lend me tuition money, and I just let you loan me a ton of it to save my butt. What a hypocrite I am, huh?"

"Please, Kurt, forget it," Emma said, putting her hand lightly on Kurt's leg.

He took a sip of the coffee. "I just want to

repeat what I said to you before. They arrested me for a crime that I didn't commit."

Emma kept her gaze on Kurt's tired and drawn face. "I know. I believe you," she said. "But I just don't understand how this could have happened!"

Kurt got a sheepish look on his face. He ran his hand over the stubble of beard on his chin. "You remember during the party we took a walk on the beach and looked at that house next to the Lawrences'?"

"Yes," Emma replied.

"Well, after you left, I walked down the beach for a while. Then I came back to the house, and . . . and I did something stupid," Kurt admitted.

Oh God, he got someone else to break into the house, Emma thought. *He didn't actually do it but he helped!* But she kept her tone even when she spoke.

"What's that?" she asked.

"I had been thinking—obsessing, really—about how rich all the summer people on this island are. I wanted to see how these people live—I was sure their house was filled with all these amazing things. So I went back to

the house. It's like I couldn't help myself."
Kurt paused, his eyes downcast. "Remember I told you that they use it so infrequently? Well, I didn't think they were coming up this weekend. But the sliding glass door was open," he continued in a low voice, "and I went in."

"Oh, Kurt!" Emma cried. "Your fingerprints must be all over everything!"

"That's what the cops said," Kurt replied. "But the point is, I didn't break in and I didn't take anything! I left everything just the way I found it!"

"Then someone else must have burglarized the house after you were in it," Emma concluded. "But someone saw you leaving the house. So no wonder the police arrested you."

Kurt nodded glumly. "I suppose they would consider it trespassing, anyway," he said.

"You need to tell Jane about this, you know," Emma told him.

"I know," Kurt said in an exhausted-sounding voice. "I should have already."

This is horrible, Emma thought frantically. *Unless we find the person who actually committed the burglary, Kurt's in big trouble!*

"Kurt?"

"Yes, Emma?"

Emma bit her lower lip before she spoke. "Are you sure—absolutely certain—you didn't take anything? I mean, on impulse or something?"

"Of course I'm sure!" Kurt exploded. "How could I face you otherwise?"

"Kurt, I'm not doubting you," Emma said. "It's just so unbelievable that all this is happening. But you know I believe in you." Emma took Kurt's hand in her own and caressed it gently.

Kurt was on the verge of tears. "How can this be happening to me?" he cried.

"I don't know," Emma responded, "but I'm with you all the way." She kissed him gently on the forehead.

Just then Jane Hewitt came out into the backyard with her briefcase. Kurt stood and thanked her again for helping him at the arraignment.

"Don't thank me yet," Jane said. "We've got to get started putting together a defense for you while the evidence is still fresh."

"What do I do?" Kurt asked.

"Exactly what I tell you to do," Jane

replied. "We'll start now, with you telling me everything you remember about last night." Jane took her yellow legal pad out of the briefcase and switched on a portable tape recorder.

Emma stood up. "I'll leave you two so you can work," she said.

"Why don't you go upstairs and get some sleep?" Kurt suggested. "You must be beat."

Emma smiled at him. He was so sweet, worrying about her despite everything he was going through. "I don't think I could," she told him honestly. "Besides, I promised Sam and Carrie that I'd meet them for lunch at the Play Café. I'm going to head over there now—unless you need me for something, Jane," she added.

"No, the kids are out back with Jeff," Jane said. "It's fine."

"Thanks, Jane, you're the best," Emma told her employer. "I won't stay too long."

When Emma arrived at the Play Café, Sam, Carrie, and Darcy were already sitting and laughing together at the girls' customary table.

"Hey, girlfriend," Sam called out when

she saw Emma. "Darcy was just telling us about the Masons' plans for next Halloween in their spook house. It sounds like a riot!"

But the smile had left Darcy's face. "Something terrible's happened," she said, her eyes alert.

"You're right," Emma said, sitting in the empty chair.

"What's wrong?" Carrie asked. "You look awful."

Emma took a sip from the glass of water on the table in front of her, and within ten minutes had spilled out the whole story of the party, Kurt's arrest, the arraignment, and Kurt's impassioned insistence that he had nothing to do with the crime. Her friends listened, astonished and horrified.

"The worst thing is," Emma finished, "that even though I believe him when he says he didn't do it, there's one small part of me that wonders if he was involved somehow." Emma looked down at her white-knuckled hands and tried to relax. "I hate myself for thinking that!"

Darcy, who'd been nibbling on a roll, spoke up. "Emma, you don't have anything to worry about. The only thing Kurt's stolen is your heart."

"How can you be so sure?" Sam challenged her. "Emma says his fingerprints were on everything."

"I just know," Darcy said matter-of-factly.

"What are you, psychic?" Sam asked.

"Not exactly," Darcy answered. "But sometimes I—"

"Oh, jeez," Sam interrupted her. "Look who's coming." She pointed to the door, where Lorell Courtland and Diana De Witt were breezing in, carrying their tennis racquets and dressed in designer tennis outfits.

"I know them," Darcy said, rolling her eyes. "I met them on the boardwalk a couple of weeks ago, when I was out with Molly. The dark-haired one looked at Molly as if she shouldn't be allowed out in daylight. They're one level down from cockroaches."

Lorell and Diana spotted the girls and made a beeline for their table.

"Well, well," Diana said to them sarcastically, "if it isn't the rest of the Aqua-Man gang." Diana had derisively nicknamed Kurt Aqua-Man the summer before.

"Oh, too funny, Diana," Sam replied. "Go crawl back under your rock."

"Now, now, let's not be nasty," Lorell

trilled. "Emma, honey, I think maybe your boyfriend should stick to lovin' instead of glovin'!"

Diana cracked up, and Lorell smiled at her own cleverness.

"Of course, if Kurt had thought to wear gloves," Lorell continued, "he might be eatin' lunch with y'all right now, instead of chowing down jail food on Alcatraz."

Oh, no, Emma thought. *Somehow they found out about Kurt. It's going to be all over the island by this afternoon. That's the last thing Kurt needs!*

"Don't look so pale, Emma." Diana's voice dripped with false sincerity. "I know that the members of the Aqua-Man gang take care of each other. I'm sure that Kurt will get the best defense money can buy. You can afford it," she added pointedly.

Darcy looked directly at Diana. "Instead of worrying about Kurt, maybe you should worry about not using a condom last night," she said conversationally.

Emma watched Diana's face turn white. For a moment the girl was too stunned to respond. Evidently Darcy was right! Emma looked at Darcy in wonder. How had she known?

"How did you find out about Kurt?" Carrie broke in.

Diana brightened. "When everyone's talking about something, it's hard to avoid listening," she answered sweetly.

"It's important to be friends with your local police," Lorell put in. "One of the nice officers told us about it. With so many dangerous criminals walkin' the streets of this island, you can't be too careful!"

"He didn't do it," Emma shot back at her.

"That's not for you to decide, is it?" Lorell asked. "Diana, I think we'd better take our leave and let this little club continue its meeting. Bye, y'all!" Lorell and Diana went to find a table of their own.

Emma rolled her eyes.

"Those girls are hateful," Darcy said.

"You got that right," Sam replied.

"But what can we do to help Kurt?" Carrie asked.

"There are only two things to do," Darcy said.

"And they are?" Sam inquired.

"Simple," Darcy said. "First, find the real burglar. Second, get the judge to sentence him to life in prison with Diana and Lorell!"

EIGHT

That evening Emma chose a booth at Rubie's Café, near the old fishing village. Rubie's was owned by Kurt's self-proclaimed adoptive mother and was not frequented by summer residents. Kurt had explained to Emma earlier that afternoon that he preferred to meet there rather than at one of the more popular island establishments.

"Everyone's already looking at me like I'm Charles Manson or the guy who shot the President to impress Jodie Foster," Kurt had said over the phone. "I'd rather meet on my home turf."

He looks exhausted! was Emma's first thought as he walked toward her. She was stunned at Kurt's haggard and drawn appearance. *I've never seen him like this*. He slowly walked straight to her booth, trying not to notice a couple sitting at the counter who pointed at him and whispered as he walked past.

He saw them, Emma thought, *and he's trying to pretend he didn't. But I can tell*.

"Hey, gorgeous," Kurt said quietly, sliding tiredly into the booth, "I missed you this afternoon."

Emma smiled and brushed a wisp of hair out of her eyes. Her hair was held back with a pair of black sunglasses perched atop her head, and she'd chosen a simple pair of form-fitting blue jeans and a yellow silk tank top. She'd made an extra effort—she wanted to look great for Kurt's sake.

"I missed you, too," Emma murmured, and leaned across the table to kiss him gently on the lips.

Kurt kissed her back. "That's a lot more fun than spending the afternoon with your lawyer."

"What did you and Jane talk about? You look so tired!" Emma asked with real concern.

"No kidding," Kurt agreed. "After spending all night in jail, I got a crash course in criminal procedure from your boss. Law's a lot more relevant when you're the person wearing the handcuffs!"

"I don't doubt it," Emma said understandingly, taking a sip of water. She could hear the gentle slapping of the surf against the pilings outside the restaurant as they talked.

"There's no way I can thank Jane enough for what she's doing for me," Kurt said. "She knows I can't afford to pay her."

"I don't think she cares about that," Emma said.

"Well, she's amazing," Kurt said gratefully. "She's got pages and pages of notes. Then we drove out to the beach so she could see the scene. Then, after she dropped me at the country club, she said she was going home to start writing motions."

"Motions?" Emma asked, puzzled.

"Legal motions," Kurt explained, taking Emma's hand as he spoke. "For example, a defendant is allowed to ask the prosecutor for all kinds of information, and the prosecutor has to hand it over. Stuff like witness lists."

"I don't know very much about these things. I've never had a reason to."

"Me neither," Kurt said, caressing Emma's fingers. He stared out the window at a couple of lobster boats pulling into their moorings. "Until now."

A waitress came over and took their orders. Kurt ordered a bucket of steamed Maine clams, and Rubie's special broiled cod fillet.

How could I possibly eat? Emma wondered, but she forced herself to order.

"I'll have a cup of clam chowder and the crab cakes," Emma said.

The waitress wrote down their orders, and then seemed to linger just a moment, staring at Kurt, before heading to the kitchen.

"What's she staring at?" Kurt asked. "Have I grown an extra nose or something?" He fell silent, his face a mask of fatigue, anger, and confusion.

"I know this must be very hard for you," Emma said sympathetically.

Kurt ran his fingers through his hair in frustration. "The worst part is that the club's suspended me without pay until my trial. There goes my summer job!"

"Oh, no!" Emma cried.

"Oh, yes," Kurt retorted. "They said it would be too controversial for me to keep working there now. I guess they think their members would be horrified at having a criminal suspect teach their kids how to swim. Maybe they're afraid I'm a child molester, too!"

"That's just not fair!" Emma protested.

"But guess what? It's perfectly legal. I asked Jane," Kurt said grimly. "It's legal for everyone to treat me like I'm a leper, and it's also legal for people to think I'm guilty until I prove myself innocent. It's not fair, it's not right, and it's against what America is *supposed* to be all about, but it's legal."

Emma said nothing. What could she say? Their dinners arrived, and they both picked at their food for a while. Evidently Kurt was having just as tough a time eating as Emma was.

Finally he threw down his fork and crumpled up his napkin. "Let's get out of here," Kurt said. "I need some sleep."

They each laid some money on the table—

Kurt was too tired to protest Emma's paying for her own dinner—rose, and left. When someone catcalled "Bye, Jesse James!" as they went though the door, they didn't turn around to see who it was.

No one was home when Emma returned to the Hewitts' house. There was a note saying that they had all gone to the movies and wouldn't be back until late.

Thank God, thought Emma. *I'm too exhausted to make polite conversation or deal with the kids.* She climbed the stairs to her room and headed immediately for the bed. She lay staring at the ceiling awhile. *None of this seems real*, she thought. *I don't know if I can handle it.*

"You can handle it," she answered herself out loud, as if to talk herself into it. It didn't work. She felt on the verge of tears. Then she realized that it was Kurt she would normally go to if she was upset, that he would hold her and comfort her—but now it was her job to comfort him.

"What I need," Emma murmured out loud, "is a shoulder to cry on." But whose? Her first choice would have been her Aunt

Liz in New York City, but she knew her aunt was in Europe on business.

I'll call Carrie, Emma decided as she got up and undressed, hanging her clothes in the closet. Then she slipped into a silk kimono and sat down on the bed to dial Carrie's number. *Just talking to her will make me feel better.*

But there was no answer at the Templetons'. She tried Sam next, but Mr. Jacobs said that Sam was out with the twins.

Emma hung up the phone feeling even more depressed. *What should I do?* she wondered, at a total loss as to how to make herself feel better. Suddenly she was tempted by the thought of a glass of wine—it would relax her. But she shook her head resolutely. She wasn't going to allow herself to use wine as a crutch, as she had started to do a few months earlier. There had to be another way.

The diary! That's it! She opened the small drawer in her nightstand and pulled out the tapestry-covered journal that her aunt had given her before she came to Sunset Island the previous summer.

Why can't my mother be more like her

sister Liz? Emma thought for a moment. *Aunt Liz has a worthwhile job running an environmental organization, she has boyfriends who treat her with genuine respect, and she listens to me when I talk to her. She's everything my mother isn't.*

Emma hadn't written a word in the diary since the summer before. She opened it and scanned some of her entries from a year ago. As she read them she smiled and shook her head. *I've come a long way since then in some ways*, she realized. *At least that's good news.* Then she took out her favorite calligraphy pen, opened the diary to a fresh page, and began to write.

I can't believe a year has gone by since I've written in this journal. Last summer, I wrote in it a lot when I felt confused, which seemed to be most of the time. Kurt and I are still together, but last night he got arrested for a burglary even though he didn't do it. And when he told me that he was innocent, I doubted him! A tiny part of me, deep deep inside, still doubts him. I tell myself I love him—I know that I love him. Then how can I be suspicious of

*him? What does that make me? Here's
Kurt being treated like some kind of
common—*

The phone rang in Emma's room, interrupting her writing.

"Hewitt residence," Emma answered automatically, putting her calligraphy pen back in its case.

"Emma darling, it's your mother!" said the girlish, enthusiastic, well-bred voice on the phone.

Oh, great, Emma thought, closing her eyes. *My mother is the last person in the world I want to talk to right now.*

"Hello, Mother," Emma said tonelessly.

"Always so formal!" Kat chided. "Listen, darling, I have wonderful news!"

"Great, Mother, tell me," Emma said without enthusiasm.

"I'm on Sunset Island!" she exclaimed happily. "I'm staying at the Sunset Inn. I decided to come up a couple of days early to get myself in the mood for the party! Isn't that grand?"

"Grand," Emma repeated tonelessly.

"You know I love this island of yours," Kat babbled. "So say something, darling!"

"Something," Emma repeated.

Silence. Finally Kat spoke. "I don't know why you want to ruin this for me, Emma. You're very hard for your age, do you know that?"

"I'm sorry, Mother," Emma said with a sigh. Why did her mother always bring out the bitch in her? "I've just had a rough day, that's all."

"I don't doubt it," Kat replied. "I'm very concerned about you, dear. I just read the most shocking story in that little local newspaper about how you had to bail your boyfriend out of jail after he got arrested for burglary!"

Oh, no, Emma thought wildly. *It's in* The Breakers! *Now not only can people talk about it, they can read about it.*

"He's innocent, Mother," Emma said.

"But darling, it's right there in the paper!" Kat exclaimed.

"It says he was arrested," Emma shot back. "It doesn't say he's guilty!"

"Cresswells don't associate with criminals," Kat reprimanded her daughter, as if she hadn't heard a word that Emma had said. "I hope this doesn't interfere with my party."

Her party? She's worried about what effect this will have on her party? Emma couldn't take any more of this.

"Mother, it seems to me that both of us are having boy problems at the moment. It's a pity yours are worse than mine," she said, her voice venomous.

"I don't understand," Kat said in her usual gay tone. "What on earth are you talking about?"

"What I mean is this, Mother," Emma said. "My boyfriend may have been arrested, but he isn't guilty. But your boyfriend, the one and only Austin Payne, the man you are planning to marry, spent last night in the arms of a girl my age right here on the island!"

"You always do this, Emma," Kat said in a small voice. "You lash out with lies and try to hurt me. You know that story about Austin isn't true."

"Just like it wasn't true last summer?" Emma asked her mother. "You didn't believe me then, either, until the truth got shoved in your face." The summer before, Kat had actually caught Austin with another woman, after accusing Emma of lying when Emma told her that he was cheating on her.

"That was then, this is now," Kat said evenly. "We're here for our engagement party. Things are quite different."

I'm so sick of her calling me a liar! Emma cried inside. "Don't you get it, Mother?" she said, her voice harsh with pain and turmoil. "Austin was practically molesting Diana De Witt at a party last night!"

"Emma, I am not going to listen to this blathering nonsense about the man who's going to be my husband!"

"It's true, Mother," Emma said quietly.

"It's nonsense!" Kat said, her voice cracking. "And I don't intend to let you hurt me again!"

Emma heard the click of the receiver as the phone went dead in her hands. *So she's hung up on me again,* she thought. Emma was surprised to find tears streaming down her face as she hung up her phone.

Well, I told her the truth, Emma thought. *Carrie would say that the truth sets you*

*free. What I want to know is, why don't I feel
any better?*

But there weren't any answers, only the
tears that fell as if they would never stop.

NINE

Emma awoke with a start. The room was pitch-black. Her clock told her it was past midnight. After crying for what seemed like hours, she'd fallen into a dreamless sleep without ever getting under the covers.

She crawled under the covers and closed her eyes, but now that she was awake all her problems flooded her mind again, making sleep impossible.

Okay, then, she thought, throwing the covers back off, *I'll go for a walk until I'm too exhausted even to think anymore.*

She got up, pulled on some sweatpants and a sweatshirt, and laced her feet into some Nikes. Then she headed downstairs and out to the beach.

Don't think, she commanded herself as she put one foot in front of the other.

Twenty minutes later, the sound of a voice shook her from her trance.

"Emma! Is that you?" a voice called from the boardwalk.

Emma looked up to see the outlines of two young women, one walking, one in a wheelchair.

"Hi," Emma said, going over to Darcy and Molly. "I certainly didn't expect to see anyone out here at this time of night."

"Neither did we," Molly said snippily. "That's why we came."

"We have a fondness for the witching hour," Darcy said with a smile. She gave Emma a look of concern. "Couldn't sleep, huh?"

"I'm exhausted," Emma said, falling into step with Darcy, Molly working the controls of her electric wheelchair. "I know I need to sleep, but I can't seem to stop my mind from working overtime."

"It's terrible about Kurt," Molly said.

Emma looked over at her with surprise. This was the first civil thing she had ever heard Molly say.

"I know Kurt from the country club," Molly continued, brushing some of her wind-swept brown curls from her cheek. "After the accident, he arranged for me to use the pool when the club was closed. He's a good guy."

They walked—and wheeled—along in silence for a moment. "I feel so . . . so inadequate," Emma finally said. "If I could buy him his freedom, I would."

"But you can't," Darcy said knowingly.

"No," Emma agreed. "Money won't do it this time. Jane won't even take any money for defending him."

"She probably knows what a good guy he is, too," Molly said.

"Thank you, Molly," Emma said gratefully. This was a whole other side to Molly, and she liked this one much better.

"You know what's really terrible?" Emma continued. "So many people who should know better are perfectly willing to believe Kurt is guilty."

"It's partly because he's poor, I think," Darcy said thoughtfully. "Some people just love to judge other people on the basis of economics. I should know."

Emma looked at Darcy's face in the moonlight and waited for her to continue.

"Hey, let's stop for a while," Molly suggested. "It's hard for me to hear you two when this stupid chair is going."

They stopped and sat on a bench overlooking the ocean.

"You were saying?" Emma prompted Darcy.

"I come from what people call the wrong side of the tracks," Darcy explained. "My dad was sick for quite a while and couldn't work, and my mom had to support six kids on a waitress's pay. It was tough."

"I can imagine," Emma murmured.

"Kids called us white trash because we got our clothes at the Salvation Army one year. And this girl started a rumor that I'd slept with every guy in school even though I was about the only girl around who was still a virgin."

"That's really terrible," Emma sympathized.

"What's terrible is that everyone believed her because I was poor and powerless." Darcy flicked her long black hair away from her face. "See, it's not so different from how things are with Kurt. I was guilty unless I could prove myself innocent, and that's what's happening to him, too."

"There are a lot of very screwed-up, cruel people in this world," Molly added bitterly.

"Anyway, enough moping," Darcy said firmly. "What we need to do to help Kurt is to come up with an action plan."

"We?" Emma repeated.

"Molly and I talked about it," Darcy said. "We want to help any way we can."

Emma smiled and thanked them.

Darcy stood up and looked out at the ocean. Then she turned to Emma. "Sometimes I get . . . feelings about things, know what I mean?"

"Not really," Emma admitted.

"On our way over here, Molly and I went by the house that got burglarized," Darcy continued. "Molly hung out on the boardwalk for a while and I went down to the beach behind the house and just stood there for a minute. I got a very creepy feeling, like whoever is involved in this is really messed up. And the whole thing has something to do with revenge. Does that mean anything to you?"

"Not a thing," Emma admitted. She stared hard at Darcy. "Are you telling me that you . . . I don't know . . . have powers or something?"

Darcy shrugged. "Sometimes I just get these feelings. I know things. And other times," she said with a shrug, "*poof*—absolutely nothing!"

"I've seen her do it," Molly confirmed. "It's very weird. But that makes her fit right in to my very weird household!"

"I have an idea," Darcy said. "How about if we meet tonight, go over all the facts, and see if we can't brainstorm this out?"

"We can meet at my house," Molly said. "My parents are at a horror-movie convention in Florida." She rolled her eyes.

"That would be great," Emma said, "if I can get the time off. Would it be okay if I invited Sam and Carrie?"

"I don't want anyone else to come," Molly put in quickly.

"I really think you'd like them, Mol," Darcy told her.

"And they're good friends of Kurt's," Emma added. "You'd be helping him if you'd say yes."

"Well, okay," Molly finally agreed. "But I don't want them to think they have to be, like, buddy-buddy with me, or something. It's just a meeting to try and help Kurt. Agreed?" Molly put out her hand for Emma to shake.

"Agreed," Emma said, shaking on it.

"Come about seven," Molly said, putting her chair into gear.

"We can order pizza," Darcy said. "You haven't lived until you've seen the look on the delivery person's face when our butler opens the front door!"

"You're sure it's okay if I go out?" Emma asked Jane again. "You and Jeff have been canceling your own plans a lot lately to take care of the kids, and I know that's my job." It was six-thirty Sunday evening, and Emma was getting ready to leave for Molly's house. She had called Sam and Carrie in the morning, and both had enthusiastically agreed to meet at Molly's house that evening. Then she'd spent the day with the three Hewitt kids at the country club— which had been a depressing experience without Kurt there. Jane and Jeff had told her three times that it was okay for her to go out, but she still felt guilty.

"Emma, go," Jeff said gently. "We told you, it's all right."

"This is not exactly a normal situation," Jane added, putting down the book she was reading. "I know you want to do everything you can for Kurt."

"Mommy, Ethan and Wills won't let me play!" Katie cried as she ran into the den.

"Come on up here, young lady," Jeff said, scooping up his daughter. "I'll read you a book."

"But your book doesn't have any pictures," Katie said, making a face.

Emma laughed, kissed the little girl goodbye, and headed out the door. To her surprise, she found Trent Hayden-Bishop just pulling into the driveway in his flashy convertible.

"Hi there," Trent said, sticking his head out of the window.

"If you came to gloat about Kurt, I'm not interested," Emma said bluntly.

"You cut me to the quick, Emma," Trent said in his nasal Boston tones. "I told you, I've changed."

"Meaning you're not a weenie anymore?" she asked sweetly.

"If I was a weenie, why did you go out with me for so long?" Trent asked pleasantly.

He had a point: They'd spent a lot of time together over the years. And she had to admit he *was* handsome. But the new, more enlightened Emma found him superficial and boring. Still, she had changed, so maybe he really had, too.

"How's Daphne?" Emma asked, changing to a more neutral subject.

"She's great," Trent answered. "She's really gotten her life together in the past year, you know? Actually, she's the reason I'm stopping by. She asked me to tell you that we'll do anything we can to help Kurt get out of this mess."

Emma put her hands on her hips. "Trent, this is very hard for me to believe."

"But it's true," Trent insisted, flipping his long forelock out of his eyes. "Daphne would be with me now, but she's in bed nursing a cold."

Emma looked into Trent's eyes and, difficult as it was for her to believe, all she saw was sincerity.

"Thanks," Emma finally said. "I'm sure Kurt will appreciate the sentiment."

"I would have told him myself, but we're not exactly pals," Trent said dryly. He reached for Emma's hand. "If he's your guy, I know he must be okay."

Emma took her hand out from under Trent's. "Thanks again," she said. "Listen, I've got to go. We're having a powwow at the Masons' house to see if we can figure out some way to help Kurt, and I'm running late."

"The Masons' house?" Trent asked in surprise. "That bizarre haunted place on the hill? I didn't think anyone lived there."

"Well, you thought wrong," Emma said. Distant thunder rumbled from far away. "Better put your top up," she said. "It's going to rain."

"Ciao, Em," Trent called as he hit a button that raised his convertible top. "Fight the good fight!"

She waved back and got into the Hewitts' car. She pulled out behind Trent and watched him zoom off down the street. She wanted to believe that Trent was telling her the truth. Right now Kurt needed all the friends he could get.

Emma drove to the Masons' and parked next to the Templetons' Porsche. Since Carrie had said she would pick up Sam, evidently they were both already there.

Darcy answered Emma's knock on the giant black front door. "I see you didn't want to ring the doorbell," she said with a grin as Emma entered.

"No, I thought I could do without the screaming this evening," Emma responded wryly.

"Tell me this place isn't max!" Sam said, coming out of the kitchen.

"Let's call it unique," Emma said.

"What's truly funny is that no one really needs to use either the knocker or the buzzer," Darcy said, "because the Masons never lock the front door."

"Why should they bother?" Sam asked. "This looks like the kind of place people would try to break *out* of, not *in to!*"

"You got it!" Darcy laughed. "Come on, we're all in the kitchen." Sam and Emma followed Darcy to the back of the house. "I decided to make homemade pizza instead of ordering out."

"Her pizza is to die for," Molly said. She sat in her wheelchair in front of the counter, slicing mushrooms.

"Hi, Emma," Carrie said from her perch next to Molly. "Does everybody like extra cheese?" she asked, her knife poised over the mozzarella.

"Extra extra," Molly instructed.

Emma caught Darcy's eye and smiled. Evidently Molly was feeling comfortable with Sam and Carrie, and they were comfortable with her, too.

Thunder grumbled loudly from outside, followed by a streak of lightning.

"The storm's getting closer," Darcy said, getting some onions from the refrigerator.

"Nothing could compare to that hurricane." Carrie stopped sprinkling mozzarella on the pizzas and shuddered. "That was the scariest thing I've ever been through in my life."

When the pizzas were assembled, Darcy stuck them both in the oven and set the timer. "I was thinking that while the pizzas are baking, we can make a list of the facts that we know so far," Darcy suggested. Emma noticed that a pad and a pen sat on the kitchen table.

"Fact one," Emma began. "Kurt admits he was in the house, which is why his fingerprints are on everything."

"But he didn't break in," Carrie pointed out. "He said the door was open."

"Do the people who live there corroborate that?" Darcy asked.

"That's about the only good news we've had so far," Emma said. "Jane spoke with them, and they admitted they often don't remember to lock the back sliding glass doors. So there was no forced entry."

"What about the burglary part?" Sam asked with a frown on her face.

"And how did the police get a description of Kurt?" Carrie wondered.

"So far none of the missing jewelry has turned up," Emma reported. "And as for the description of Kurt, a girl named Hillary something-or-other was at Howie's party and said she saw someone leaving the house. The person she described exactly matched the description of what Kurt was wearing—

right down to the red bandana. Jane is interviewing her again tomorrow."

"Well, so what?" Molly asked. "He admitted he was in the house, so what's the big deal about seeing him leave it?"

"She said she saw him running fast." Emma sighed. "And she says she saw him drop something in the sand, then pick it up and run even faster."

"Ouch, " Sam said with a wince. "This doesn't look good."

"I know," Emma admitted. A loud clap of thunder punctuated her statement, and rain began to beat against the windows.

"Well, I've written all that down," Darcy said, bouncing the eraser end of the pencil on the table. "The thing is, I know he didn't do it."

"We all know he didn't do it," Carrie added, looking at Emma.

Emma smiled at her. Her friends' support meant everything to her now.

"The way I see it," Darcy said, "someone is trying to frame Kurt."

"But how?" Sam asked.

"And why?" Carrie added.

"Tell them about that strange feeling you

got when you walked past the house that was burglarized," Molly urged Darcy. "You've only told me and Emma."

"It was a very weird—and, I have to admit, scary—feeling," Darcy said in a low voice. "I got a feeling that—"

Just at that moment, a tremendous rumble of thunder erupted, lightning flashed crazy shadows on the walls, and all the lights went out.

"Oh, damn, a powerline must have gone down somewhere," Darcy said. "Molly, reach into the drawer by the phone and see if there are any candles there."

There came the sound of a drawer being opened and rummaged through.

"Zip," Molly reported.

"I was afraid of that," Darcy said ruefully. "That means the only candles in the house are upstairs in the storage room."

Everyone was quiet for a moment. "Is there a flashlight, maybe?" Emma asked.

"My parents are not exactly the well-prepared type," Molly said. "Besides, they'd think a blackout was hilarious. They'd be doing their best to scare each other to death right about now."

"Gee, fun couple," Sam said into the darkness.

The rain pelted down even more loudly against the house.

"I guess I should try to feel my way upstairs to find the candles," Darcy finally said, getting up from the kitchen table. "Everyone else stay right here."

"Yeah, like we were going to move," Sam replied, gulping hard. "This house is unbelievably creepy in the dark."

"There's nothing to worry about," Darcy assured everyone. "I'll just go—"

"No one move!" a harsh voice rasped from the doorway.

Everyone in the room screamed in fright. Sam practically jumped into Emma's lap. Emma could just make out a dark figure standing at the entrance to the kitchen. A ski mask covered the person's face. Her heart pounded in her chest, and she grabbed Sam with shaking hands.

"Here's a tip," the muffled voice growled from behind the ski mask. "Quit sticking your nose in other people's business!" Then, as quickly as the figure had appeared, it disappeared into the shadows of the front hall.

For a moment no one could speak, no one could move.

"Di—did that really just happen?" Carrie asked in a quavering, hushed voice.

"Yes, unless we're all having the same hallucination," Molly said in a tight voice.

Suddenly a realization dawned on Emma. "We were being warned off Kurt's case," she said. "If only we could have caught whoever that was!"

"Get real," Sam said. "This is not some movie-mystery script where you miraculously catch the bad guy and live to tell the tale. Some freak just came after us, and this is for real!"

"Sam's right," Darcy agreed. "I sensed something crazed in that person, whoever it was. We could all be in real danger."

TEN

The late-morning sunshine glinted through the window of her bedroom as Emma gave herself one last look in the mirror and then smiled humorlessly. *How should one dress to eat lunch with one's mother and her fiancé, whom one detests?* she thought mockingly, giving her straight blond hair a final brush. *Maybe I'll spill soup on them both; that would be fun.* But Emma knew she was too polite to carry out that plan. *Too bad I'm not Sam!* she lamented. *She'd do it in what Pres would call a "New York minute."*

Early that morning, Emma had found a note scrawled by Ethan the night before. The note read: *Emma—your mother called. Says come to lunch with her and Awstin at*

Sunset Inn tomorrow noon. Ethan. Though her heart sank when she read it, Emma had cracked up at how Ethan had misspelled Austin's name, and she'd made a mental note always to spell it Ethan's way.

At least Emma was pretty sure she'd chosen the right outfit for lunch. She wanted to wear something that was proper enough that her mother wouldn't bitch, but different enough that she would give it a second thought.

So Emma had picked out of her closet a gorgeous, nearly backless Italian white cotton sundress. *Very haute couture,* she thought, *perfect for Kat. But what will Mother, who absolutely loathes politics, think of the political button I'm about to accessorize it with?* And Emma pinned on herself a large badge that read *COPE: The Future of Sunset Island.*

Thus outfitted for battle, Emma—who had promised to babysit next Saturday evening in exchange for time off that day— borrowed the Hewitts' second car and drove the few miles to the Sunset Inn. Emma pulled the car into a vacant spot, got out, and walked through the lush lobby of the inn and out through the sliding glass doors to the open-air restaurant that overlooked the ocean. Emma had been to the deck restaurant before, but once again she was struck by how awesomely beautiful it was in the summer sunshine. There was a gentle breeze blowing toward shore, and a woman was running on the beach trying to get a kite aloft, her small daughter running and jumping behind her. *That looks like fun,* Emma thought with a sigh. *Why didn't my mother ever do that with me?*

"Emma, darling! Over here!" Emma heard Kat's girlish voice calling to her. She turned toward the sound and saw her mother waving and straining like an anxious second grader trying to get her teacher's attention. Sitting across from Kat at a table set for three was Austin Payne. His hair was slicked back in a perfect ponytail. He wore a black T-shirt under a wide-shouldered black Italian jacket, and he had his usual smug smile on his face.

I loathe him so much, Emma thought again. *All he's after is my mother's money, and it looks like he'll have all he wants in a few months.*

Emma unenthusiastically walked over to her mother's table, suffered through her mother kissing her on both cheeks as if she and Kat were back in Europe, and shook Austin's hand politely.

"Great to see you again, Emma," Austin said, pulling out Emma's chair.

"Oh, likewise," Emma said, knowing her tone belied the words.

"Emma," Kat said, still in her girlish tone of voice, "I simply adore that lovely dress you're wearing—Alaia's the designer, no?— but what is that silly pin you have on?"

Score: daughter one, mother zero.

"It's a political pin, Mother," Emma said matter-of-factly, adjusting the button pinned below the shoulder of her dress.

"I know *that*," Kat responded brightly. "I wasn't born yesterday. Why, when I was in college, the students were constantly wearing those tiresome buttons. So why are you wearing one now?"

Austin spoke up. "It's a COPE button, Kat," he said with a mischievous grin. "If you wear one, it helps you deal with the world better. And right now I could deal with a visit to that buffet over there."

146

Austin pointed to a long series of tables covered with platters and chafing dishes as he snickered at his own joke.

What a marginally talented, quasi-artistic, fake little snot he is, Emma thought. She smiled politely.

"Actually, Mother," Emma said, ignoring Austin, "COPE stands for Citizens of Positive Ethics."

"Well, good for you, dear," Kat said, obviously neither knowing nor caring what her daughter was talking about. "I'm simply ravenous, darling, aren't you?" she asked Austin, running her French-manicured nails lightly over his forearm.

"Let me get you a plate," Austin told Kat, pushing back his chair. "Shall we, Emma?"

Austin filled two plates of food, one for himself and one for Kat, while Emma selected her own lunch from the array of dishes. *I can't believe she lets herself be treated like such a baby*, she said to herself angrily. *How is he supposed to know what she wants to eat?*

When Emma and Austin returned to the table, Kat's eyes twinkled at her young fiancé. "How can I think about food when watching you walk across a room is so delicious?"

I'm going to throw up, Emma decided. She forced herself to eat a few bites of overcooked broccoli quiche and turned back to her mother.

"You want me to tell you about COPE now, Mother?" she said with a smile.

"I'm sure it's lovely, dear," Kat said, patting her collagen-plumped lips with the edge of her napkin. "But let's talk about something more fun. I know! The party!"

"But I want to tell you," Emma insisted, knowing that COPE was the last thing her mother wanted to hear about. "COPE is an organization that's trying to protect the island from overdevelopment and also help some of the poor people who live here. There *are* poor families here, you know."

"Yes, I know," Kat said with a real note of sympathy in her voice. Emma's heart leapt. *Does my mother have an actual conscience she's kept hidden all these years?* "The Bloodworth family has a house out here and they took a terrible beating in the stock market recently," Kat continued. "It's a true pity."

Austin laughed heartily as Emma tightened her grip on her fork. "I don't think that's the kind of poverty Emma is talking about, Kat," he said.

I know what he's doing, Emma said to herself. *He's trying to form some kind of alliance with me by showing me that he's cooler than my mother. Well, he won't succeed!* "Just forget it," she snapped.

"Actually, what Emma says is true," Austin went on. "An artist friend of mine with a summer house on the bay side told me about them. COPE did a lot of good work here after Hurricane Julius struck, right, Emma?"

Emma nodded grudgingly. So he knew about COPE. Big deal.

"They rescued a lot of people stranded during the storm," Austin continued. "I heard they even saved May Spencer-Rumsey's photo collection from a flood in her mansion! Including an original David Frohman worth hundreds of thousands of dollars!"

I'm sure he wishes he'd been there, Emma thought nastily. *Because if he had been, I bet that David Frohman photograph would have disappeared. He'd have sold it to some snooty art dealer friend and then never had to marry my—*

Emma sat up straight, a feeling of shock coursing through her body. *Is it possible that Austin's the one who stole the jewelry the night of the burglary and then tried to frame Kurt for it? And he doesn't intend to marry my mother, but is only sticking around for the engagement party to cover his tracks?*

"Emma, are you all right?" Kat asked. "All of a sudden you're very pale!"

Okay, I've got to play it very carefully now, Emma thought. *I can't let on what I'm thinking.*

"It must be something I ate, Mother. Don't worry," she said, forcing a smile to her lips. "Let's talk about something less depressing than that hurricane."

"What a good idea, darling!" Kat trilled in approval.

"Are you all ready for the party, Mother?"

Kat brightened. Emma saw that this was the right subject for discussion. Kat spent several minutes giving a blow-by-blow description of her party planning, invitation list, and seating plan.

"And what about you, Austin?" Emma asked her mother's fiancé sweetly. "How have you been keeping yourself busy lately?"

"Oh, doing this and that," Austin replied, taking a sip of coffee. "Painting some."

"That's nice," Emma said blithely, lifting her teacup. "I'm glad you've found time to work, what with your busy social schedule."

"Oh!" Austin laughed easily. "I thought that was you at that party the other night at what's-his-name's house."

"Howie Lawrence," Emma answered pointedly, glancing at her mother.

"Yes, that was fun," Austin continued. "I stopped in with an artist friend of mine, Shane Levine. The Lawrences just bought one of his paintings, so he thought it'd be cool to drop by."

"I understand completely, darling," Kat said, giving Emma a frosty look.

"Hey, guess who I ran into there?" Austin asked. "That couple from Marblehead's daughter—what was her name? De Twitt?"

"De Witt!" Kat said brightly, nodding at Emma as if to say *I told you so!* "Diana is their daughter. Such a nice girl!"

"Exuberant, anyway," Austin went on. "She practically forced me to dance with her. I left right after that," he added casually.

Maybe he's telling the truth and maybe he isn't, Emma thought. *What's more important is that he just went to the top of my suspects list for stealing the jewelry. He's low enough to do it, I know he is.*

After lunch, Emma went back to the Hewitts' to pick up Katie for her afternoon swimming lesson at the country club. It was so depressing to be there without Kurt that she hurried Katie away after her lesson. On the way out she saw Daphne and Trent lying next to each other by the pool, holding hands, and she walked by as quickly as she could. *Once life was that simple for me, too,* she thought sadly.

"Hey, Katie, want to stop and see Kurt?" Emma asked Katie impetuously as she pulled the car out of the country club's parking lot. Katie had really been missing her favorite swimming teacher. And of course, Emma missed him even more.

"Yeah!" Katie cried, jumping up and down in her seat. "At his house where he lives?" she asked.

"That's right," Emma said with a smile, heading the car toward the other side of the island. She took a shortcut that Kurt had taught her, and was there in a matter of minutes.

The front door was open when Emma and Katie arrived. "Anybody home?" Emma called inside. No one answered. "I think it's okay if we just go in, since the door's open," Emma told Katie. *I only wish that had been true for Kurt,* she reflected wryly, thinking of the burglarized house.

Holding the little girl's hand, Emma walked into the Ackermans' modest living room. She expected to see Kurt watching television or just moping about his fate. But Emma quickly saw she was wrong. He had a visitor.

It was Darcy.

What's she doing here? Emma wondered, immediately thinking the worst. *That's all I need—my new friend has a big crush on my boyfriend. She* is *his type, and she's certainly not rich like me,* Emma thought bleakly. Then she scolded herself. What reason did she have to think that Darcy Laken was making a play for Kurt? Why did she immediately want to treat her as guilty?

Because they both come from the same background, they share a similar history, and because confident Darcy can deal with Kurt's problems a lot better than I can, Emma thought sadly. She sighed and went into the room.

"Emma! Katie!" Kurt said, smiling broadly. "What a great surprise."

"I hope so," Emma said. She didn't feel quite sure.

Kurt turned to Darcy. "Please excuse me for the next thirty seconds," he said. Then he marched over to Emma and gave her a 1930s-style dip kiss.

Darcy laughed and applauded. "Well done!"

Emma blushed and smiled happily. "That's quite a welcome," she said.

"Me, too!" Katie piped up, holding up her arms to Kurt.

"You, too!" Kurt agreed, lifting the little

girl and giving her an extra loud smack of a kiss on the cheek.

"I miss you at swimming," Katie told Kurt gravely.

"I miss you, too," Kurt said, setting her down.

"We've been going over the story of the burglary again and again," Kurt told Emma. They sat down on the couch and Katie immediately jumped into Kurt's lap. "Darcy stopped by to help me," he added, pointing to a stack of file cards on the table.

"How's it going?" Emma asked them.

"I don't know," Kurt said honestly. "There's got to be a clue somewhere as to who really stole the jewels!"

"Maybe this will mean something to you two," Darcy said. "After that guy tried to scare the life out of us last night, and after you all left, I helped Molly to bed, and then I went to sleep myself—" she began.

Emma gave a little laugh. "I'm so glad we finally discovered that the guy had only flipped the circuit breaker at the fuse box and we could get the lights back on. The whole thing was petrifying!"

"Darcy told me about what happened,"

Kurt put in. "I think you guys should have called the police."

"We talked about it," Emma said. "But we figured they'd just say we made it up because we're your friends. You know, to try and get you off the hook."

"Even the police are already convinced I'm guilty." Kurt sighed.

"Listen to me," Darcy said firmly. "I had a very strange dream last night, and I want to know if it means anything to either of you."

"No offense, Darcy," Kurt said, "but what do dreams have to do with this?"

"Sometimes I know things," Darcy said. "I can't really explain it. Sometimes things come to me in a flash, and sometimes in a dream."

"What did you dream?" Emma asked, tucking her feet under her.

"The thing is, I don't remember all that much of it. But it was kind of like when I stood near the burglarized house the other night. In the dream I was on the oceanside beach. Someone was yelling the word *revenge* over and over again. There was a huge flash of light. And then I woke up."

Emma listened, transfixed. "What do you think it means?" she asked.

"I have no idea," Darcy admitted. "I hoped you or Kurt might."

"Listen, Darcy," Kurt said, running his hand through his hair, "I know you're trying to help. But I really don't believe in all that new-age psychic stuff."

"It's not new-age stuff to me," Darcy said simply. "It's something I've been able to do all my life."

"Well, then, why can't you just divine who the real criminal is?" Kurt asked skeptically.

"I wish I did know who the thief is," Darcy said. "But I don't have any control over what I know or when I know it."

"Well, the dream doesn't mean a lot to me now, but I'll think about it some more," Emma promised, "and see if it rings any bells." She stood up and lifted a half-asleep Katie from Kurt's lap. "I've got to get this kid home for her nap. Kurt, can you walk me out to my car?"

"Sure," Kurt said. They walked outside.

"Kurt, I realize I never got a chance to tell you this, what with everything that's happened, but my mother and Austin are having a big engagement party tonight," she said softly, so as not to wake the little girl. "I'd really like it if you would come there with me."

Emma could see Kurt wince. "Kurt?"

Kurt shook his head. "Any other time, Emma, you know I'd be happy to go," he told her bluntly. "But tonight? They'd all be laughing at me! The party would be about me, not about your mother and Austin!"

"That's not true!" Emma answered him, her voice full of love. "I want you to come. But I can understand why you would be reluctant," she admitted.

Kurt smiled at her. "Thanks, Emma," he said gratefully. "When this is all over, I promise I'll make us a private party you won't believe."

Emma smiled back. But for a fleeting instant, she had a vision of Kurt in prison clothing, and she hoped that his party for the two of them wouldn't take place behind bars.

"Okay," Emma said. "I'll look forward to it. I'll ask Carrie and Sam if they'll come with me tonight." Kurt opened the car door, and Emma carefully placed Katie in the front seat and buckled her in. Then she put her arms around Kurt and gave him a sizzling good-bye kiss. *Just to make certain he'll think about me when he's back in there with Darcy*, she told herself.

She drove home quickly. "You don't have any worries, huh, little girl?" she said softly to the still-sleeping Katie. "You could sleep anywhere."

"My baby got tuckered out, eh?" Jeff said when Emma walked in carrying Katie. "I'll take her."

"Thanks," Emma said, handing Katie to her father.

Emma went upstairs and dialed Carrie's number. *I hope she and Sam can come with me tonight*, she thought, crossing her fingers for luck. She absolutely did not want to go to this thing alone.

Carrie, fortunately, was home, and readily agreed to come to the party.

"Thanks a million, Carrie, you're a lifesaver," Emma said.

"Hey, what are friends for?" Carrie said warmly. "Want me to call Sam for you?"

"Would you?" Emma said. "I've got a zillion things to do."

"Sure," Carrie agreed easily. "You know Sam—she's always up for a party."

"This one may be dreadful," Emma warned.

"Well, she'd also do anything for you," Carrie added, "so it really doesn't matter. I would, too, you know."

"I know," Emma said, a lump forming in her throat. They were really the two best friends anyone ever had.

Emma hung up and went back downstairs to help Jane with the picnic she was preparing, but her mind was somewhere else completely. She kept thinking about Darcy's dream. Revenge. But what in the world did it mean?

ELEVEN

"Emma? Telephone for you!" Jane Hewitt's voice echoed up the stairway and into Emma's room, where she was in the final stage of dressing for her mother's big engagement party.

Emma glanced at the clock. Seven-fifteen. She was supposed to meet Carrie and Sam at the entrance to the Sunset Country Club at eight. *Whoever this is, it's going to have to be a short conversation*, Emma thought quickly. *It's probably Sam calling to tell me that my outfit is too conservative. And she doesn't even know what I'm wearing.*

"Hello?" Emma said into the phone as she checked her pantyhose to make sure she didn't have a run.

"Hi, it's Daphne Whittinger," came the voice through the phone.

Daphne Whittinger! Emma was astonished. *That's just about the last person I would expect to call me.*

"Hello, Daphne," Emma said politely. "What can I do for you?"

"Oh, Emma," Daphne said, a touch of shame in her voice. "I'm so nervous about calling you, after last summer and everything. But I looked up the Hewitt's number in the directory anyway."

"Don't worry about last summer," Emma said. "You . . . well, you had some problems. It wasn't really your fault. I'm just glad you got some help."

"I'm so happy you feel that way!" Daphne said feelingly. "You're so much more together than I am."

Emma smiled ruefully. *Her opinion on that subject would change really fast if she saw my diary.*

"Anyway," Daphne continued breathlessly, "Trent and I were thinking about what we could do to help Kurt. So we decided to give a party to help raise money for his defense."

"That's really nice of you," Emma said, almost speechless with surprise. "But Jane Hewitt—that's Kurt's lawyer, my employer—won't take any money."

"Oh," Daphne said, silent for a moment. "Well, I know Kurt got fired from his job at the club, so I'm sure he can use the money we'll raise."

"He didn't get fired, he got suspended," Emma corrected her.

"Right," Daphne agreed quickly. "Anyway, we're planning this for tomorrow night at the Play Café, and we hope you'll come."

Daphne and Trent giving a party to help Kurt? Emma felt like she'd stepped into an episode of *The Twilight Zone*. She actually pinched herself to be sure she hadn't fallen asleep and started dreaming.

"Well, that's . . . that's really nice of you," Emma managed.

"We think it's a crime that people are treating him like dirt," Daphne said. "I bet it makes you feel awful."

"It does," Emma said honestly.

"And I'll bet a lot of people are treating *you* like dirt just because you're his girlfriend," Daphne said.

"I really don't pay any attention to that," Emma said, surprised at Daphne's bluntness.

"Well, we want to show our support. So will you be there?"

"Yes, of course I'll come," Emma said.

"That's great!" Daphne cried. "I really want to see you."

"Well, it will be nice to see you, too," Emma replied, hoping she sounded sincere.

"Look, I've got a lot more phone calls to make, and a bunch of things to do," Daphne concluded. "So I'll see you tomorrow night, eight o'clock, Play Café. Bye!"

Emma said good-bye and hung up the receiver. *Will wonders never cease?* she thought. *Next Diana De Witt will show up and say she's planning to go work with Mother Teresa in Calcutta.*

Emma turned her full attention to her clothes and makeup, having a bare thirty minutes before she had to meet Carrie and Sam at the country club. It being a characteristically cool Maine summer evening, Emma had selected a sleeveless fitted black sheath with a mock turtleneck, and wore a very short matching jacket over it with black braiding banding the sleeves.

You look entirely too respectable, she thought, and made a face at herself in the mirror. In defiance she got out a pair of ankle boots with a high, narrow heel and slipped them on her feet. *Much better,* she thought, surveying her image. *Mother would expect some tasteful pumps with this ensemble.*

Happy with how she looked, but dreading the idea of spending an entire evening with her mother, her mother's egocentric young boyfriend, and their fake friends, Emma went downstairs, said good-bye to the Hewitts (who all complimented her on how she looked), and drove over to the club. Travis Tritt's song "Country Club" was playing on the radio as she headed to the party, and Emma cranked the volume up, laughing at the odd coincidence.

When she drove into the country club's familiar parking lot, she saw that Kat had arranged for valet parking for the event. *How typically Kat,* Emma thought dryly as she pulled the Hewitt's car up in front of the main entrance and let one of the two uniformed valets take the car from her.

"Whoa, hot footwear!" Emma heard a low female voice call out from behind.

She whirled around and smiled at Sam. Carrie stood directly beside her. They looked terrific, Emma thought happily. Carrie wore a navy pleated miniskirt with an oversized pink sweater, while as usual Sam took a fashion risk—and succeeded—by pairing a black catsuit with a cropped orange denim jacket covered in rhinestones.

"Where'd you get that jacket?" Emma asked as Sam twirled around to show it off.

"Isn't it great?" Sam said. "I got the whole outfit on loan from the Cheap Boutique. I talked the manager into making me a walking advertisement tonight. I've got to return everything tomorrow."

"Sort of like Cinderella," Carrie said, laughing.

"How did you talk him into it?" Emma asked.

Sam waved her hands. "Don't ask!"

"Let's just say she has a date with a certain boutique store manager who has a hopeless crush on her," Carrie explained, rolling her eyes.

"You are one of a kind," said Emma, shaking her head.

"Too true, too true," Sam agreed breezily. "Now, what do you say we go show 'em how it's done?"

The three girls strode together into the country club's main lounge. Emma saw most of the men in the room glance their way with interest. *We must really look great,* she thought. Then she took a quick look around the room and laughed. *It's because we're about the only ones here under the age of thirty!* Kat had told Emma at lunch that she was chartering a plane to bring some of Austin's art-crowd friends in from New York, but evidently they hadn't yet arrived.

"Wow! Look at this place!" Sam exclaimed, taking in the opulent surroundings. "If this is how the rich and famous party, I'm ready to be rich and famous!"

Emma and Carrie smiled. It really did look spectacular, if a little hokey, Emma thought. Kat had chosen an art theme for the engagement party, and had decorated the walls of the lounge as if it were an art gallery. Every other painting was a print of a famous artwork by the likes of Rembrandt, Seurat, and Picasso. And mixed in with them were original paintings by that rising American *enfant terrible* of the art world, Austin Payne.

"Uh-oh, Emma! Parental unit approaching at twelve o'clock!" Sam muttered, cocking her head toward Emma's mother.

Kat came over to the girls, bussed Carrie and Sam like long-lost daughters, and then thanked them gushingly for coming to the party with Emma.

"I'm so proud of her," Kat told Emma's friends, putting her arm around her daughter. "Not only is she my daughter, but she's my best friend."

You don't know a thing about me, Emma thought, but she vowed to be civil to her mother at the engagement party. "Thank you, that's very nice of you, Mother," she said.

"I think of her more as a sister than a daughter," Kat confided to Sam and Carrie. "And everyone says I look more like her sister, too!" she added gaily.

"I think there's a big crowd of people

arriving," Emma said diplomatically, pointing to the doorway. Sure enough, a gaggle of bizarrely dressed men and women was coming through the door.

"Oh! Those are our friends from Manhattan," Kat said with a big smile. "The *crème de la crème* of the art world."

"And he looks very *crème*-y," Sam said, staring at a gorgeous guy in faded jeans and a tux jacket.

"I must go greet them," Kat said, excusing herself. "Emma, be an angel and go into the back room and fetch my antique pocket watch for me, will you? I told Arthur Boozer all about it—it's gallery-quality, you know, and he collects watches—and I see he's just arrived."

"Sure, Mother," Emma answered. "Where is it?"

"In the pocket of my wrap—the gold silk one from Paris," Kat explained, heading toward her friends. "Thanks ever so much, darling!"

When she had gone, Sam, Carrie, and even Emma started giggling. Soon it became uncontrollable laughter.

"In seven words, Emma, your mother is a piece of work!" Sam exclaimed.

"I know," Emma said ruefully. "Believe me, I know. Listen, can you two take care of yourselves for a minute? I've got to go get that pocket watch for her."

"No problem," Carrie said. "I'll walk Sam over to the food. That'll keep her occupied for a while, right, Sam?"

"You betcha," Sam joked. "I haven't eaten since dinner!" Emma laughed. Sam was known for her voracious appetite and her ability to eat without gaining a pound. Carrie had once suggested that scientists study her to learn her secret.

"Great," Emma said. "I'll meet you over there in a minute."

Emma threaded her way to the back cloakroom. *There it is*. She quickly spotted her mother's wrap. The garment was draped across a chair in the back of the room, right next to a black cashmere jacket that Emma recognized as Austin Payne's.

Emma reached into the pocket of the wrap and easily found the pocket watch. But as she was taking it out she accidentally knocked Austin's jacket to the floor. She reached down and picked it up. Out of the pocket fell a red bandana. Emma stared at it a moment. A red bandana. Where had she seen a red bandana? And then it came to her. "It's just like the one Kurt was wearing the night he was arrested!" Emma exclaimed. "I knew Austin Payne was involved, I just knew it!"

Quickly, before anyone else could come into the cloakroom, Emma fished around in Austin's coat. From the inner pocket she pulled a piece of paper. She unfolded it. It read: *Bangor, Tuesday. 438 Brewer Road. See Joey in afternoon. Bring items.*

With trembling fingers, Emma folded the note back up and put it back just as she'd found it. *Obviously he's the thief*, she thought, hurrying back to the party. *This fellow Joey must be a fence who's going to buy the stolen jewelry. Austin's planning to sell it tomorrow!*

Emma searched for Carrie and Sam and found them dancing with two middle-aged men. When the song was over, Emma motioned her friends over to her. They were only too happy to get away.

"Come with me, I've got incredible news!" Emma whispered.

Sam and Carrie followed Emma out onto a secluded terrace, where Emma filled them in on her discovery of the note.

When Emma was finished talking, Sam whistled. "Do you know what you just did?" she said excitedly. "You just cracked this case!"

"I don't know for sure," Emma cautioned, glancing around to make sure Austin didn't walk out onto the terrace unexpectedly. But in her heart, she was sure.

Carrie spoke up. "There's only one thing to do. We have to follow Austin to Bangor and catch him red-handed," she said emphatically but quietly, her eyes darting from side to side, watching for Austin. "No police officer is going to arrest him on the basis of that note."

"You're right! This is going to be just like the movies!" Sam put in excitedly.

"Ssh!" Emma said, anxious to bring the gathering to a close. "No, Sam, it's a good plan, but *we* can't do it. Even if all three of us could get the time off, which I doubt, Austin would recognize us right away."

"I guess you're right," Carrie admitted. "But then who?"

"I have an idea," Emma said. "I'll tell you in the car on the way."

"We're leaving?" Sam joked. "I haven't had a chance to mingle with the *crème de la crème!*"

Emma laughed. "Yes, we're leaving," she said. "Don't worry about manners or anything. I guarantee my mother won't miss us."

Without saying another word, Emma, Sam, and Carrie slipped away from the party. A few moments later, they were in Emma's car on the way to a certain haunted house on a hill.

Now, Emma said to herself, *I only hope that Darcy is willing to do this for me!*

TWELVE

The next morning Emma stared out the window of the Mason family's specially equipped van and marveled at the events of the past twelve hours. The day before, who would have believed that she would soon be on her way to some seedy part of Bangor to find the crucial evidence leading to the arrest of her mother's fiancé—the man who had tried to frame her boyfriend for burglary? Not to mention that her partners on this expedition would be a girl she'd met only a few days earlier—a girl who Emma thought might have ESP—and another girl in a wheelchair. When Emma really considered it, the whole thing was almost too improbable.

However, here she was, cruising along at

sixty miles an hour on the Maine Turnpike toward Bangor, Darcy Laken driving, Emma riding shotgun, and Molly Mason in the rear of the van. The midmorning sun shone through the windows of the van as they neared the town of Waterville.

"How about if we stop in Waterville for breakfast?" Darcy suggested. "Even if we take an hour to eat, we can be in Bangor by noon."

"Sounds good to me," Molly said from the back seat. "I'm starved."

"Okay," Emma agreed. "Austin's note said that his meeting is in the afternoon. We should have plenty of time."

Darcy pulled the van off the highway at the first Waterville exit. She stopped at a convenience store and came out with two big cups of coffee, a cup of tea for Emma, some cheese and crackers, and a big bag of fruit.

"I know a great place for quick picnic," she told Emma and Molly as she restarted the van.

"Someplace private?" Molly asked nervously. Emma watched her compress her lips with anxiety. Evidently she still hated the idea of people staring at her in her wheelchair.

"No," Darcy admitted. "But it's really nice. You game?"

It took a moment for Molly to answer. "Yeah," she finally said.

Minutes later, Darcy drove them onto what looked to Emma like a college campus. They were on a hill, and Emma could see a stunning vista of the Maine countryside, no matter which direction she looked in.

"This is beautiful," Emma marveled. "Where are we?"

"Colby College," Darcy said. She drove past the library, a big building with huge white columns that faced a broad lawn.

"I didn't know you meant a picnic at Colby!" Molly exclaimed. "I don't want to eat here. All those rich, snotty kids . . ." she began, her voice trailing off.

Emma winced. *That means people like me*, she thought, embarrassed.

"That means people like you, Emma," Darcy said with a laugh, saying out loud exactly what Emma had been thinking.

"But I'm really not like that," Emma protested.

"Oh, I think maybe you were—but that was before you let evil people like me and Sam and Carrie and Molly corrupt you!" Darcy teased her.

"How about if we just park and eat in the van?" Molly suggested.

"I don't think anyone will stare at you, Molly," Emma said.

"That is total bull," Molly retorted.

"She does speak from experience," Darcy agreed.

"Point taken," Emma murmured.

"Believe me, most kids think nothing bad can ever happen to them," Molly said bitterly. "So they look at me like I'm some kind of weirdo."

"So prove you're not," Darcy suggested, stopping the van in a parking lot across from the open, grassy area.

"I don't want to have to spend my life proving something," Molly snorted. "*If* you don't mind."

"So don't," Darcy said. She undid her seatbelt and turned around to face Molly in the back seat. "But actually, I think the world is much less focused on you than you seem to think it is. Other people have their own problems."

"Which are a lot less visible," Molly muttered, staring out the window.

"Agreed," Darcy said. "So what'll it be, eat here in the back of this stuffy van, or eat out there in the sunshine?"

Molly rolled her eyes. "You are such a master manipulator, Darcy."

"Thanks," Darcy said cheerfully. "Hey, Emma, grab the food, will you?" She engaged the wheelchair lift and helped Molly onto it.

Once out of the van, Darcy wheeled Molly out to the library steps, and Emma set up a simple picnic. For a few moments, Emma and her new friends ate in silence, soaking up the morning sunshine. A few students walked by, and Emma noticed that some of them looked curiously at Molly in her wheelchair. But just as Darcy had predicted, most of them were so wrapped up in whatever was going on in their own lives that they barely noticed Molly at all.

"I really want to thank you two again for coming with me to do this," Emma said sincerely as she peeled an orange.

"No problem," Darcy said. "I love a good adventure."

"Me, too," Molly admitted. "Or at least I used to. I was always the first one to want to try something on a dare—hang-gliding, sky-diving . . ."

"You parachuted out of an airplane?" Emma asked incredulously.

"Yep," Molly said, popping a cracker into her mouth. "It was awesome."

You simply cannot judge someone from looking at them, Emma reminded herself.

"Hey, Molly," Darcy said, breaking into Emma's thoughts, "did you remember to bring extra film for the camera?"

"Got it," Molly said.

"Molly's going to be our lookout," Darcy explained between sips of coffee. "And I want her to take pictures in case anyone runs into trouble."

Emma nodded gravely. Darcy's words reminded her of the seriousness of what they were about to do. She had no illusions that trying to get the goods on Austin Payne was going to be simple.

"What did you come up with for a disguise?" Darcy asked Emma. The night before, they had decided that the only way Emma could possibly get near Austin would be if she was disguised; otherwise, Austin would surely recognize her.

"I've got a brown wig that I borrowed from Sam, dark sunglasses, and a ratty overcoat." She took a bite of a banana. "Oh, I also thought I'd draw a birthmark on my face with an eyebrow pencil."

"Well, either that'll work or you'll look like the world's biggest fool," Molly said with a grin.

Just then a handsome guy walked out of the library. He turned his head to look at them as he passed. But Emma saw that his attention wasn't focused on Darcy, and it wasn't focused on her. He was gazing at Molly. And Emma knew that look—it was the look that meant he thought Molly was cute.

Actually, Emma thought, *she is cute, once she gets that bitter look off her face. Her skin looks gorgeous in this sunlight, and she had the prettiest hazel eyes!*

"Hey, Mol, that guy was giving you the Look," Darcy said to Molly with a wink.

"No, he wasn't," Molly retorted. "He was

only staring at me because I'm in a wheel-chair."

"Wrong," Darcy said implacably. "It was the Look all right, wasn't it, Emma?"

"It was," Emma confirmed.

"One day," Darcy said, wagging a finger at Molly, "you'll start to notice that you get quite a few of those looks."

"Sure," Molly barked sarcastically. But Emma saw a hopeful look in her eyes, as if somewhere inside of her she believed that it could be true.

Hurrah! Emma thought. *This girl deserves someone to love her like Kurt loves me. Just because she had the bad luck to be in an accident doesn't mean she doesn't deserve love as much as anyone.*

"I think we'd better head out," Emma said, starting to gather up their litter.

"You're right," Darcy seconded. "Last thing I want is for us to get to Bangor and find out Austin's been there and gone already. Let's go!"

Sixty-five miles later, Darcy pulled the van off Interstate 95 again, and then threaded her way through the back streets of Bangor, stopping in a seedy section of town. Darcy seemed to know the streets and alleyways of Bangor like the back of her hand.

That could come in handy in an emergency, Emma thought, *though I hope we don't wind up in a high-speed chase!*

"Okay, this is it," Darcy announced, executing a parallel park a few doors down from the address that Emma had found on the note in Austin's pocket.

"Pretty seedy," Molly commented.

"And how," Darcy said.

Emma looked up and down the street. Molly was right. Brewer Road was a strip of used-clothing stores, pawnshops, fast-food outlets, and adult bookstores.

"Austin's going to be visiting that pawnshop over there," Darcy went on. She pointed to one on the opposite side of the street.

"Okay," Emma said, her voice quavering a bit. *I'm scared, I admit it,* she thought. "Let's go over the plan again."

"Sure. But it'll be a piece of cake," Darcy said.

Does this girl have ice in her veins?

Emma thought, amazed. *Nothing fazes her!*

"We wait here until Austin arrives," Darcy continued. "When he goes in, Molly and I casually go in after him."

"I'm coming, too," Emma said quickly.

"Are you sure that's a good idea?" Darcy asked.

"I'm sure," Emma said firmly. She pulled the ratty brown wig out of a bag and began fitting it on her head.

Molly stared at Emma. "You look like a reject from one of those grade-B women-in-prison movies," she said.

"Good," Emma said. "Austin would never expect that of me, not in a million years. I'll be invisible."

"I hope so," Darcy said, looking at Emma skeptically as Emma dotted a big birthmark on her face with her eyebrow pencil. "Lose the birthmark," she added, making a face.

"You stay in the van until you see him, and then give us the signal," Molly reminded Emma. "I'll make sure I get some photos."

Darcy nodded. "When Austin leaves, we'll play it by ear from there. The big thing is to see if the jewelry he fences is stolen."

"Then let's do it," Molly said.

Darcy got out of the van and helped Molly down. Together, they idled along Brewer Road, pretending to window-shop in the windows of the various pawnshops and junk stores along the road. Meanwhile, Emma kept a careful lookout for Austin from inside the van, twisting the ring on her finger anxiously.

Just as she was checking her ratty disguise in the rearview mirror, Emma noticed with a start that an expensive black car had pulled up in front of the pawnshop. *Oh my God, that's my mother's car!* Emma thought, her heart pounding in her chest. *Austin's not going to much trouble to make himself inconspicuous.*

Emma opened and shut the van door quickly, the signal that she had prearranged with Darcy and Molly to indicate that Austin had arrived. But there was no need—the other girls had already noticed the car. All three watched with fascination as Austin got out of the car, looked hurriedly back and forth, and skulked into the pawnshop.

This is it! This is really it! Emma thought breathlessly as she hurried to catch up with Darcy and Molly. The three of them followed Austin inside as inconspicuously as possible. Darcy pushed Molly up and down the aisles of pawned merchandise for sale, while Emma sidled toward the back of the shop. All of them, however, could hear Austin as he talked to the store's proprietor.

"I brought the items," Austin said to the short, balding man in an ill-fitting suit. He glanced around the store furtively, and Emma ducked behind a display of used guitars.

"Yeah?" the bald man said, scratching his protruding stomach.

Austin reached into his pocket and pulled out a manila envelope.

The jewelry! Emma thought.

The proprietor studied Austin and said, "Let's go into the back room, where I can get a better look at it. Pete, you take over here," the store owner said to a young man who was pricing pawned mechanic's tools.

Emma watched as the two men disappeared into the back room. She saw Darcy motion to her—*she wants to meet me outside to talk*, Emma thought. *Well, there's not a lot I can do in here now, anyway*, she reasoned. Darcy and Molly left the store, and Emma met them back in the van a few moments later.

"What do we do now?" Emma asked, a note of panic in her voice. "Can't we just go in there and make a citizen's arrest?"

Darcy laughed. "You've watched one too many television shows, Emma," she said, shaking her head.

"Yeah, that could get us killed," Molly added.

"So what do we do?" Emma cried. "We're so close!"

"Sit, watch, and remember that you catch more bees with honey than you do with vinegar," Darcy said firmly. "Just wait. I have a idea."

"This better be good," Molly muttered.

The girls sat in the van and watched as Austin finally came outside and then got into the car. Emma watched him take off.

"Okay, let's go, Emma," Darcy said, getting out of the van.

"Where?" Emma asked, completely bewildered. "He's gone!"

"Why, back inside, obviously," Darcy said. "And take off that dumb disguise. Molly, you wait here, this'll only take a second." Darcy marched off into the pawnshop again. Emma followed.

Emma watched, astonished, as Darcy went right up to the proprietor and struck up a conversation with him about some jewelry that was displayed in a showcase. She listened as a slightly flirtatious Darcy steered the discussion around to the weather, and then to local Bangor politics. It turned out that the guy and Darcy's family belonged to the same church and knew a lot of the same people.

"So who was that rich guy who left your shop just as I was coming in?" Darcy asked in an offhand way.

"Who knows with these types?" the bald man said with a shrug. "One of those rich out-of-staters—only he isn't rich now." He guffawed. "He pawned a gold ring and some diamond cufflinks."

A gold ring? Emma thought, puzzled. *Diamond cufflinks? I don't recall those being on the list of things stolen from the house.*

Emma casually sidled up next to Darcy. "Excuse me, I couldn't help overhearing you," she said in a friendly voice. "I'm thinking about purchasing a gold ring for my boyfriend's birthday. Could I possible see it?"

"A-yuh. I'll be right back," the man said, apparently thinking that he might be able to turn a quick profit.

But if he's fencing stolen goods, why isn't he more suspicious? Emma thought as she waited for the man to return. She caught Darcy's eye. Her friend appeared to be thinking the same thing.

"Here you go," the man said when he returned. He spread out a piece of velvet on the counter, opened his hand, and let fall a bejeweled man's ring.

Emma picked it up. It somehow looked familiar to her. She peered at the inside and saw the engraved initials *A.P. & K.C.* Then it dawned on her. This was the ring that her mother had given Austin several months ago! The initials were Austin's and her mother's! This ring had absolutely nothing to do with the robbery.

"Well?" asked the clerk. "Do you want it? It's yours for two thousand dollars."

"Uh, I don't think so," Emma stammered.

"Think it over," the man coaxed. "How's

eighteen hundred? The fellow who pawned it says he's using the money to buy a present for his fiancée. A-yuh, a romantic. And I can see you're a romantic, too, young lady— wouldn't this ring make an extra-special gift?"

Austin pawned that stuff so he could buy my mother an engagement present? Emma thought miserably. *We did all this for nothing?*

"If you don't like this one, I've got others," offered the bald man, anxious to make a sale.

"Maybe another time," Emma said, now in a hurry to get back to Sunset Island. She rushed out the door. Darcy said a casual good-bye and followed soon after.

"How'd it go?" Molly asked when Emma and Darcy got to the van.

"A total waste," Darcy answered in a dejected tone. "Emma, can you drive back? I'm feeling beat." Emma nodded and took the keys. Darcy gave her directions back to Interstate 95, stayed awake until they got on the highway going south, and then promptly fell asleep. Emma saw Molly starting to drift off, too. *Did Austin really go to all that trouble just to buy my mother an engagement present?* Emma asked herself, incredulous. She switched on the radio to keep her company as the miles rolled under the wheels.

Darcy suddenly bolted awake and screamed, "Oh, no!"

"What is it?" Emma asked, looking over at Darcy.

"Are you okay?" queried a stunned Molly.

"It's that dream again, that same dream," Darcy explained, wiping perspiration from her brow. "I was on the beach. Someone yelled 'Revenge!' over and over again. There was a huge flash of light. This time, I could see the glint of a knife. Then I woke up."

"What do you think it means?" Molly asked.

"I haven't a clue," said Darcy quietly. "Don't you have *any* idea, Emma?"

"None. It makes no sense at all," Emma said with a sigh. She stared out at the ribbon of highway ahead of her and wondered if anything would ever make sense to her again.

THIRTEEN

"But Kurt, the party is for you!" Emma said into the phone. It was Tuesday evening, and Kurt had just called to tell Emma he wasn't going to the party at the Play Café.

"That's exactly why I don't want to be there," Kurt responded. "It makes me feel like a charity case."

"It isn't like that!" Emma protested, twisting the phone cord around her finger in consternation. She had left a message for him the day before. They hadn't had a chance to speak, but Emma had never expected this response.

"Well, it feels to me like a pity party," came Kurt's tense voice through the phone. "I just can't deal with it."

"But isn't it kind of rude of you not to come?" Emma questioned.

"Rude?" Kurt exploded. "I'm supposed to be concerned about being rude? I'm worrying about my life right now, Emma, not about being well-bred!"

"You're right," Emma said softly. "I understand."

"Hey, I'm sorry, babe," Kurt said in a low voice. "I'm taking my frustration out on you, and you're the last person in the world I want to do that to."

"It's all right," Emma assured him. She took a deep breath and exhaled, trying to rid herself of some of the tension and anxiety that had plagued her ever since this nightmare began. *But I have to be strong for Kurt's sake*, Emma told herself. *It's just that I'm so scared for him!*

"Why don't you stop by here after the party?" Kurt suggested. "I miss you."

"I will. But maybe you'll change your mind?"

"Don't count on it, sweetie," Kurt said gently.

Emma hung up and finished dressing for the party. *Life is so ironic*, she thought as she slipped a white rayon T-shirt over her head. *Just when people like Trent and Daphne are coming around to being decent human beings, Kurt won't even be there to appreciate it.*

"Stinky Stein got braces! Stinky Stein's a Frankenstein-mouth!" Emma heard Wills chanting as she ran down the stairs. Thirteen-year-old Stinky Stein lived next door and was Ethan's best friend.

"So? Big deal," Stinky spat back at Wills. "At least my braces will come off. Your ugly freckles will last a lifetime."

"Yeah, just like Grandma's liver spots!" Ethan hooted, pointing at Wills's face.

"Oh yeah? Oh yeah?" Wills searched for a truly great insult.

"Hey, guys, chill out," Emma said lightly.

"You look kinda nice," Stinky said, obviously trying not to stare at Emma too hard.

Wills picked up on this right away. "Frankenstein-mouth likes Emma! I bet you want to kiss her!" he screamed with glee.

"Shut up, you little moron!" Stinky yelled, and both he and Ethan went after Wills.

"Excuse me, guys, we don't allow murder

in this house," Jeff said, coming up behind Stinky and catching his arm just as he was about to punch Wills.

"Bye!" Emma called to them as she headed for the front door. She was thrilled to leave their squabbling behind her. *Kids have no idea how easy they have it*, Emma thought.

When she arrived at the Play Café, it was already hopping. The Flirts were up on stage playing a tune that Billy had written for Carrie. As Emma worked her way through the crowd by the front door she saw a large box on her left. *The Kurt Ackerman Defense Fund* read a sign over the box. Emma peeked inside—it was already half full of bills. A warm feeling flooded her heart. It was so wonderful to know that most people really did care about Kurt, really did believe that he was innocent. If only there was some way to prove it!

"Hey, girlfriend," Sam said, coming up next to Emma. "Great turnout, huh?"

Emma nodded. "I wish Kurt had come with me to see it," Emma said.

Sam raised her eyebrows. "He's not coming? That's a drag."

"Oh, you know Kurt." Emma sighed. "He's just so proud—he feels like it's charity or something."

"Bogus," Sam commented. "Hey, guess who's here? Molly came with Darcy!"

"That's great!" Emma exclaimed, her eyes scanning the crowd. "Where are they?"

Sam led Emma across the room to a table where Darcy sat next to Molly. A cute guy with auburn hair and a University of Michigan sweatshirt sat next to Molly. They were deep in conversation.

"Hi, there!" Darcy said happily when she saw Emma.

"Oh, hi," Molly said, looking up. "Great party," she added, then went back to talking to the guy.

Emma smiled at Darcy, who smiled back. Molly was really coming out of her shell!

"You're not going to believe this, but the bitch contingent actually showed up for this gig," Sam yelled over the music. She pointed to the dance floor, where Diana De Witt and Lorell Courtland were dancing with two preppy-looking guys wearing sunglasses.

"What total hypocrites," Emma marveled.

"I can think of a few choice words that are worse than that," Sam added drolly.

"How about Wills's favorite new insult?" Emma suggested. "Toilet-breath."

"Works for me," Sam agreed with a laugh. "I'm going over by the stage where Carrie is so I can stare up at Pres while he's playing and think dirty thoughts." Sam waved goodbye."

"Emma! How terrific of you to come!" Daphne Whittinger exclaimed, touching Emma's arm.

"It's great that you did this, Daphne," Emma said.

"Oh, it's the least I could do," Daphne said, her eyes shining. "After last summer and all."

"I told you, Daphne, that's in the past."

"You are really an amazing person," Daphne said. "I admire you so much."

"I don't think I'm very amazing, but thanks," Emma said, laughing.

"Emma, you're looking marvelous," Trent said, joining Daphne.

"She always looks marvelous," Daphne added.

"Enough compliments!" Emma said playfully, holding up her hands.

"How about a spin around the dance floor, then?" Trent asked. "For old times' sake. You don't mind, do you, Daphne?"

"Why, of course not," Daphne assured him. "It's perfectly understandable."

"Such a mature girl," Trent said, leaning over to kiss Daphne's cheek. "Shall we?" He extended his hand to Emma.

Oh, what the hell, Emma thought. *Trent really is an old friend, and everything else is completely in the past.* She took his hand and moved into his arms.

"The Flirts sound great," Trent said, moving easily to the ballad Billy was singing.

"They are great," Emma agreed. She looked up at Trent. "You know, I think it's so nice that you got together with Daphne."

"She's very sweet. A bit intense, though," Trend added. "But we're having fun."

Fun. That sounds like Trent, Emma thought. *Trent has never taken anything seriously in his entire life—except fun.*

"Speaking of fun, I take it that's what you and Kurt are *not* having these days, eh?" Trent inquired.

"How could we?" Emma asked. "It's like some horrible nightmare. I just can't believe this is happening!"

Trent nodded sympathetically. "And you're a girl who should be having fun, Emma. I've always thought that. We had fun once, didn't we?"

"I suppose we did," Emma conceded.

"Kurt takes life entirely too seriously," Trent said. "You were hardly raised for that."

"But that's not how it is at all!" Emma protested. "I love him, Trent! If only I could find the real thief, I could clear Kurt's name!"

Trent moved close. "Here's a little piece of advice from an old friend," he said in a low voice, his breath tickling her ear. "Don't stick your nose into other people's business if you want a happy life."

Emma stopped dancing and stood frozen on the spot. *"Don't stick your nose into other people's business." That's what the sinister voice behind the ski mask warned us at Molly's house! Oh my God—it was Trent! And he framed Kurt!*

Emma backed away from Trent, her eyes wide with fear.

"What is it?" Trent asked.

She spun around, frantically searching for a way to escape. She had to get away from him! She had to have time to figure out what to do! Without thinking, she ran toward the open glass doors that led to the deck.

"Emma, don't run away from me!" Trent demanded.

But she did run, down the steps that led to the beach, her breath coming in rapid gasps of fear. As her feet hit the sand she heard footsteps behind her, gaining fast.

Was it Trent? She couldn't see in the dark, and she dared not turn around to confront him. Who knew what he might be capable of?

But no matter how fast she moved across the sand, she could hear the heavy breathing of someone moving closer.

Too late, she realized how stupid it was to run away from the protection of the crowded club. Now she was too far away even to yell for help. No one would hear her.

I've got to run up to the road, Emma thought frantically. *I've got to get help!*

But as she changed direction, intending to run uphill toward the road, she stumbled in the sand. *No!* she screamed inside her head. *He'll catch me!*

"Are you okay?" a concerned-sounding female voice asked, helping Emma up. It was Daphne.

"Daphne!" Emma cried with relief. "Oh, Daphne, I'm so glad to see you!"

"I saw you run out the back of the club," Daphne said. "You seemed really upset."

"Oh, Daphne, it's so awful!" Emma sobbed. "I found out who framed Kurt! It's Trent!"

"Trent?" Daphne repeated. "Really?"

"Yes!" Emma exclaimed. "Oh, I know you must feel terrible, and I'm so sorry, but he's really sick! He needs help!"

Daphne smiled serenely at Emma. "Oh, no, you have it all wrong."

"No, I don't," Emma insisted. "He . . . he just repeated something to me that he said when he threatened us at Molly's house. It was him all along!"

"He threatened you?" Daphne echoed. "He wouldn't threaten you. He loves you. Everyone loves you." Still she smiled, as if she had all the faith in the world that Trent was innocent.

"Oh, Daphne, I can't explain now," Emma cried. "We've got to go—"

"But you're not going anywhere," Daphne interrupted in that same placid tone.

"What are you talking about?" Emma said, pushing her windblown hair back from her eyes.

"Do you think I don't know what was going on all the time I was away?" Daphne asked Emma. "Did you think I'd stop thinking about what you did to me just because they stuck me in some hospital?"

Emma looked into Daphne's eyes and saw a gleam of madness in them. She realized with a start that what until just a moment ago had seemed to her like serenity was covering a sick and murderous rage.

"Daphne, no," Emma said softly. Her eyes darted around the beach, trying to decide which way would offer her the best chance of escape.

"Oh, yes," Daphne said, moving closer. "Emma Cresswell the beautiful, Emma Cresswell the perfect," she crooned. "Only I know you're not so perfect. I know the lies you tell about me."

"No, Daphne, it's not true," Emma said, trying to keep her voice normal. "Let's go back up to the club and—"

Daphne let out a crazed scream. "It's time for you to die!"

Daphne lifted her right hand out of the pocket of her skirt. Emma gasped. A knife glinted in the moonlight, a slashing light bolting toward her throat.

"No!" Emma screamed. She feinted to the left, dodging Daphne's swinging arm.

But madness seemed to give Daphne superhuman speed. Just when Emma thought she had gotten away, she felt Daphne's hand grab her hair, pulling her down into the sand.

"Revenge!" Daphne screamed. She raised her hand again, the knife poised to slice the life from Emma's pulsing throat.

But from out of nowhere strong arms tackled Daphne from behind, tumbling her into the sand.

"Darcy!" Emma screamed. "She has a knife!"

Emma watched in horror as Daphne

threw herself at Darcy, forcing her to the sand. Now Daphne was raising her hand to plunge the knife into Darcy. Emma grabbed at Daphne's hand to stop her. She saw the knife pierce her flesh, saw the blood begin to well up against her white skin, as if it were happening to someone else.

Darcy managed to get up, but Daphne pivoted to come at Emma again. "Die!" she screamed.

Darcy pushed Daphne's shoulder, forcing her away from Emma. Then she pulled her fist back and punched Daphne in the jaw with all her might. The knife tumbled from Daphne's hand and she fell to the sand, out cold.

"Oh my God, oh my god," Emma repeated in shock. She looked at Darcy, then found herself embracing her friend as hard as she could.

"It's okay now," Darcy said quietly, holding on to Emma as hard as Emma was holding on to her.

"Thank you, how can I thank you?" Emma babbled. She let go of Darcy long enough to wipe the tears from her face.

"I'm just so glad I got here in time," Darcy said, looking down at Daphne.

"How did you know to follow me?" Emma asked.

"I saw you leave, and I saw Daphne leave, and I got this terrible feeling," Darcy said. "Suddenly, I knew it was her. So I came after you."

Something in the sand caught Emma's eye. "Look!" Emma cried, bending down to pick it up. "A diamond and ruby necklace! This is one of the stolen pieces of jewelry!"

"She must have had it in her pocket," Darcy said.

"Now we can go to the police!" Emma cried. "We finally have proof! I thought it was Trent, but I was wrong."

"Emma?" a male voice called. A figure ran toward them from the café.

"Oh, Kurt!" Emma cried when she realized who it was. She threw her arms around him, laughing and crying at the same time. "I'm so glad to see you! But what are you doing here?"

"I decided to come to the party after all," Kurt said bemusedly. Then he saw Daphne in the sand and Emma's bleeding hand. "What the hell happened?"

"It was Daphne who did it!" Emma held out the necklace. "Look."

"I don't understand," Kurt said, pulling off his T-shirt and wrapping it around Emma's hand.

"Tell him while I go call the police," Darcy said, bending down to pick up Daphne's knife from the sand. "Watch her until I can lead the cops here. I'll be back."

"Darcy saved my life," Emma told Kurt in a quavering voice.

"What happened?" Kurt asked again, completely bewildered.

"I'll tell you everything," Emma promised, "but for right now, just hold me."

Kurt did. The nightmare was over at last.

FOURTEEN

"The whole thing is just so incredible," Sam said as she fitted a balloon onto the nozzle of the helium canister.

"I know what you mean," Emma said, looking up at the *We Love Kurt!* banner that she and Carrie had just hung over the Hewitts' front door. Daphne had confessed everything the night before, and all charges against Kurt had been dropped.

"It's amazing that no one knew how crazy she was," Jane Hewitt said, handing one end of a crepe-paper streamer to Carrie, who stood on a chair.

"Imagine—all that time she was in the hospital, almost an entire year, she was plotting to get back at Emma for some imagined wrong!" Carrie shook her head. "I mean, what is it you were supposed to have done to her?"

"Her brother told me that she told the doctor I plotted against her and stole her friends," Emma said with a shudder.

"Totally loony," Sam said, blowing up another balloon.

Carrie said thoughtfully, "Well, maybe now she can really get some help."

"What I can't figure out is how Trent could not know she was bonkers," Sam said.

"You know how oblivious Trent is," Emma said. She got more crepe paper out of the bag and handed it to Jane. "He's not exactly a deep thinker."

"And remember, she even fooled her own family," Jane pointed out. "Not that they pay any attention to her anyway," she added ruefully.

"How do the streamers look?" Carrie asked.

"Terrific," Sam said.

"It's such a bizarre coincidence that Trent used the same words when he was dancing with you that Daphne used when she tried to scare us at Molly's house," Carrie said, climbing down from the chair.

"But that's all it was," Emma said with a shrug. "Coincidence."

"Daphne has such a diabolical mind," Sam marveled. "I mean, she was kind of brilliant in her own messed-up way."

Emma nodded. "Once she saw Kurt come out of the house that night, she rushed home, put on similar clothes, and went back to commit the burglary. She knew that in the dark no one would be able to tell for sure who it was, or even whether it was a man or a woman. But everyone at the party would remember the red bandana tied around Kurt's head, and *that* a witness could see. Then after Trent came to visit me," Emma continued, "he must have innocently re-marked to Daphne that we were having that meeting at Molly's, so she knew just where to find us."

"And, she spoke in such a weird voice that we never guessed it was a woman, either!" Carrie put in.

"And all to get revenge against you and Kurt," Sam said, shaking her head.

"Well, it was Kurt who stopped her from slicing and dicing me last summer," Emma said. She looked down at her bandaged

211

hand. Fortunately, the knife had barely grazed her, and she hadn't needed any stitches.

"Mommy! Some people are here!" Katie yelled, running into the den, where everyone was decorating.

"Hi!" Darcy said, wheeling Molly in with her. "Hey, it looks festive in here!"

"I made fudge," Molly said shyly, handing a shoebox full of the candy to Jane.

"I want some!" Katie yelled.

"Not till the party, munchkin," Jane told her little girl.

"Well, then, I wish it would start now," Katie said in disgust.

"Not until Kurt comes," Emma said.

"I'll go watch for him," Katie decided, and she ran out of the room.

"Let me go find a plate for this," Darcy said, taking the fudge from Jane and heading for the kitchen.

Emma followed her. "Darcy, I can't thank you enough for what you did for me," she said.

"You already have," Darcy said, arranging the fudge on one of the serving platters that Jane had left out. "And anyway, you've helped me, too. Do you see the change in Molly? She's really starting to come around!"

"I was wondering," Emma asked, leaning against the counter, "about you being psychic. Is it wonderful or is it scary?"

Darcy shrugged. "I don't think of myself as being psychic." She licked some fudge off her finger. "Like I said, sometimes I just know things. But other times, when I really wish I knew something, I'm a total blank."

"Kurt's here! Kurt's here!" Katie screamed from the front porch.

"Excuse me," Emma said with a smile at Darcy.

"Go for it," Darcy said, smiling back at Emma with equal warmth.

Emma flew to the front hall and practically threw herself into Kurt's arms.

"I like this sort of low-key greeting," he said, grinning down at her.

"Oh, Kurt, I love you so much," Emma whispered, hugging him as hard as she could.

"I love you, too, Emma Cresswell," Kurt whispered. He bent down and kissed her.

"Kisses for me, too!" Katie begged, jumping around at Kurt's feet.

"Not this time," Kurt murmured, his gaze on Emma's beautiful, shining face. "This time is all for Emma."

SUNSET ISLAND MAILBOX

. . . *"I think the best thing about your books is how realistic they are. They're not like those books where girl likes boy, there's a little fight, girl gets boy, and everything melts away in rose-colored splendor. Emma, Carrie, and Sam have real-life problems and pressures. . . ."*

. . . *"I'm writing to tell you how much I love some books of yours—the* Sunset Island *series. They were some of the best books I've ever read! It only took me a week to finish all of them! . . ."*

. . . *"The characters seem so real that when I am reading I feel like I'm living their lives. My only disappointment is the way you ended things with Emma and Kurt in* Sunset Farewell. *Kurt brought out the best in Emma and vice versa. I hope you decide to continue the* Sunset *series, and mend things between the two of them. . . ."*

Dear Readers,

Wow! Have I ever gotten some terrific letters from you out there! It means a lot to me that you take the time to write. In fact, the letters are so great, that we're going to start printing some of them here in each book. Look for your letters in Sunset Whispers (coming out in September, 1992) and Sunset Paradise (December, 1992). I love to hear your ideas and thoughts, so keep those cards and letters coming! As always, if you'd prefer to have me answer you privately, just say so in your letter.

Write to me at:

Cherie Bennett
C/O General Licensing Company
24 West 25th Street
New York, NY 10010.

Please include your name and address, and clearly state whether you want your letter printed.

I can't wait to hear from you. See you on the island!

Cherie

Sam, Carrie, and Emma return to Sunset Island and their summer jobs as au pairs... Let the adventure begin!

By Cherie Bennett

___SUNSET HEAT #7   0-425-13383-4/$3.50**

Sam is hired by a talent scout to dance in a show in Japan. Unfortunately, Emma and Carrie don't share her enthusiasm. No one really knows if this is on the up and up, especially after her fiasco with the shifty photographer last summer. But Sam is determined to go despite her friends. . .

___SUNSET PROMISES #8   0-425-13384-2/$3.50

Carrie receives a lot of attention when she shows her photos at the Sunset Gallery. She is approached by a publisher who wants her to do a book of pictures of the island. But when Carrie photos the entire island, she discovers a part of Sunset Island that tourists never see...

___SUNSET SCANDAL #9   0-425-13385-0/$3.50

Emma has started to see Kurt again, and everything's going great...until Kurt is arrested as the suspect in a rash of robberies! He has no alibi, and things look pretty bad. Then, Emma befriends a new girl on the island who might be able to help prove Kurt's innocence.

___SUNSET WHISPERS #10 (September 1992) 0-425-13386-9/$3.50

Sam is shocked to find out she is adopted. She's never needed her friends more than when her birth mother comes to Sunset Island to meet her. And to add to the chaos, Sam and Emma, along with the rest of the girls on the island, are auditioning to be back up in the rock band *Flirting with Danger*.

For Visa, MasterCard and American Express orders ($15 minimum) call: 1-800-631-8571

FOR MAIL ORDERS: CHECK BOOK(S). FILL OUT COUPON. SEND TO:

BERKLEY PUBLISHING GROUP
390 Murray Hill Pkwy., Dept. B
East Rutherford, NJ 07073

NAME_____

ADDRESS _____

CITY_____

STATE_____ZIP_____

PLEASE ALLOW 6 WEEKS FOR DELIVERY.
PRICES ARE SUBJECT TO CHANGE WITHOUT NOTICE.

POSTAGE AND HANDLING:
$1.75 for one book, 75¢ for each additional. Do not exceed $5.50.

BOOK TOTAL	$ _____
POSTAGE & HANDLING	$ _____
APPLICABLE SALES TAX (CA, NJ, NY, PA)	$ _____
TOTAL AMOUNT DUE	$ _____

PAYABLE IN US FUNDS.
(No cash orders accepted.)